The Light of Miera

A Prelude to Light

A Short Story Collection

By Ash Hester

To Amy

thank you for being
an incredible editor &
inspiration

Love

Ash xxx

For Jacko

"Art washes away from the soul the dust of everyday life."

— Pablo Picasso

The Light of Miera
A Prelude To Light

Written by Ash Hester

First Published in 2023 by Ash Hester

Cover design by Liam Shaw Illustration based on original design by Ash Hester

ASIN (Amazon ebook): B0C172186W

ISBN-13(Amazon paperback): 9798389679139

Introduction

With the looming debut of my epic fantasy series The Light of Miera, I was strongly encouraged by Fantastic Books, my publisher, to create a mailing list and website for myself. This forced me to look at myself, my work and my career very seriously, which unsurprisingly induced a lot of doubt, anxiety and self-loathing. It did, however, unearth a plethora of unused stories and severed flashbacks from before the events of A Guard's Request.

These excerpts were intended as character development and used to practise certain writing skills, but I later went back and added to them in hopes of creating more rounded short stories. As an epic fantasy writer, the thought of writing anything with less than ten-thousand words is somewhat horrific to me, but I've never been one to turn down a challenge.

A Prelude to Light was originally planned as a tribute to the love story of my main characters, but now includes adventures and hints to build on what is to come. Each story is written to be enjoyed on its own and as part of the whole.

Welcome to Alamantra.

Ash Hester

Table of Contents

The Tournament of Hearts

Summer 3651, 24 Years BMF

* * *

Rarely did the mortals under my care realise the significance of their actions.

From my void, I would watch as they changed history for better or worse.

But not even I could predict all that was to come…

* * *

Prince Drazah commanded the attention of all who attended the opening night of the Tournament of Hearts. Having achieved his transformation and rank within the Sudran army, Drazah was now ready to take a paramour and prepare for leadership, but not just any woman could become his queen.

A young man of twenty, Drazah beamed with Sudran pride, his skin black as charcoal, his muscles taut and bulging, his transformed physique even more so. The points of the horns above his temples poked through his burnt-umber hair, and his azure eyes glittered with the promise tonight's event held.

The lavish party marked the first round of the tournament. Here, women from across the kingdom were given the chance to talk to the prince in hopes of winning his affection. Only the eight women Prince Drazah found most appealing would go through to the main event. Each eager young lady approached Drazah throughout the evening, each making various efforts to touch and charm him. They hovered around him like flies. All except the mysterious raven-haired beauty with ruby eyes, which Drazah noticed immediately.

She leaned casually against a pillar, a thin sheath dress latticed with a square pattern over the parts of her modesty. Straight glossy hair reached the small of her back and golden bracelets glistened against the dark skin of her wrists. Her ebony lips pursed to his attention, but she made no attempts to come to meet him.

Her eyes never leaving him, Drazah continued his rounds, shaking every hand. The minutes crept by and still, the woman made no attempts to win his affection, which is perhaps what made her the most intriguing person in the room. Did she not wish to become his queen? Did she already have a paramour? Fire bubbled in Drazah's belly. Was he here?

Drazah wasn't opposed to a challenge and he wasn't interested in causing a scene at his own tournament. Still, he wasn't about to let her leave without talking to him and went to ask her name.

"Nymati?" he repeated, still clumsy in his approach despite knowing the women were there for him. "Are you enjoying the party?"

"I am," she purred, making no attempts to touch him as the others had. Why didn't she wish to charm him?

"Are you?" she asked, again surprising him.

With the cocktail of feminine influences sweeping his senses, his thoughts were all over the place and Drazah wasn't sure how he felt. Between the steady stream of meat, mead and charms, Drazah was hardly sure what day it was. All he knew for certain was he enjoyed talking with Nymati.

She noticed his surprise, the corner of her ebony lips peeking into the smallest smile.

"Is that why you didn't come over?"

She continued to smile. A flurry of excitement prickled the hair upon the nape of his neck, his palms sweaty.

"Is that why you haven't charmed me?"

Her smile widened, Drazah's heart dancing in his chest.

"If I am to become queen, I wish for my king to love me, not my artes," she purred, twirling a single finger through raven hair. Her voice was so smooth it cleared his confused thoughts, leaving him with only one. "Besides, you already know who you're going to choose."

Drazah jolted. Nymati wasn't wrong, although he was surprised she knew his parents had been conspiring. There were eight places and his parents already told him who was most appropriate, the party was more of a formality. Still, the final decision was his to make.

Nymati moved in close, never touching Drazah as she whispered honey into his ear: "Or you could use it as an opportunity to clean house."

Using only the glimmer of her ruby eyes, Nymati gestured to a gaggle of four girls. The prissy, snooty, unbearable girls of more prominent families. The heiresses who walked into every room thinking they were better than everybody else for the majority of their pompous lives.

Drazah knew them well. Growing up they teased him endlessly despite his standing and, until recently, showed him little fondness. How he loathed them.

Did she know that? How could she? Who was this woman?

Was she suggesting...? Bloodlust tickled his stomach.

Nymati blinked slowly, holding his gaze with a sinister smile. Her eyes flashed blood red as she pulled away, her intent clear.

"Goodnight, my king."

My king. He liked the sound of that.

Drazah remained in awe, his mouth ajar, watching the space Nymati once filled. He wondered if she had even been there to begin with. In all his life he had never met a woman as wonderful and mysterious. There was no need for a tournament, he knew it already:

She was his queen.

* * *

The next day the entrants gathered once more in the throne hall, eager for Prince Drazah to make his announcement.

He stood upon the dais, his mother and father seated upon the golden throne behind him. Nerves rippled through his body, his eyes darting through the crowd in hopes of catching a glance of Nymati. His heart stopped as his eyes met hers across the hall.

Drazah stepped forward, announcing the names to the patient gallery.

The first three names were of his parents' choosing, but the following four he called were the four girls from the previous night and finally, Nymati.

His parents were furious but hid it well, after all, they wouldn't want people to think they fixed things. The audience buzzed as the eight girls gathered to make a row before them. Of the eight, Nymati stood in the middle of the lineup, but the rest faded into the background as Nymati turned her ruby eyes to meet his.

She brimmed with satisfaction, seizing the opportunity with a flirtatious glance, ready to prove her love in a way no other woman could. The young prince could hardly breathe, anticipation rattling his insides as his extremities firmed.

Drazah never believed it possible but now he knew it to be true: they were soulmates.

The sensation was overwhelming. His body itched and ached to be with her. How long would he have to wait until he could be close to her once more?

As was the custom, the row of girls walked toward their future king, however, Nymati did not. It was subtle, Nymati hung back as the line of hopefuls made their way forward, and Grand Master Barrick outlined the rules of the tournament.

"To prove your worth you will be required to face off against each other in rounds." The ancient Sudra could hardly keep himself upright as he croaked through the ceremony.

Nymati stopped, allowing them to leave her behind. Her eyes remained on Drazah. What was she doing?

"Entrants understand that they may forfeit their lives during each round. If you agree to these terms say aye."

Each agreed.

"I do not," Nymati called.

"What is the meaning of this?" huffed King Ushmi, but Nymati looked only to Drazah.

"My king." There it was again. "You ask me to prove my worth, but I feel I cannot show you all that I am in a challenge of such a manner. I ask that you allow me to prove myself in one match. In that one match, I promise, I will show you all that I am the only choice for queen."

"And how do you propose you're going to do that?" asked his father, but Drazah was intrigued, as was the rest of the hall.

"Sire, I am a child of the wastes. A child destined for no more than drought and starvation, yet I took it upon myself to gain entrance to the tournament. And so standing here before you, I feel I have already proven myself intelligent and resourceful, do you not agree?" The king agreed but Nymati ignored him. "And now I say I will prove myself in five more ways if His Highness would allow me but one chance.

"Firstly, I would prove my courage and have you allow me to face my seven opponents at once." This seemed to appease the congregation, but it was not unheard of, brawls were often used to open the autumn tournament in the coliseum.

"Second, I would prove my speed by not allowing one girl to lay a hand on me. Not one finger. And third, I will prove my strength by defeating each of my opponents without transforming."

Drazah shifted with the buzz of excited mumblings from the crowd in the hall behind her. It was considered a mark of disrespect to refuse your transformation to an opponent in Sudra. They were taught there was wisdom and honour in holding their strength, but only those of immeasurable power could hold their own in the face of another's Demon Form.

"Fourth, I will prove my resolve by defeating them all without moving my feet even an inch from the place I now stand. And finally, I will prove my determination and honour by vowing to remove my name from the running should I fail in but one of these tasks."

The line of girls turned to face Nymati as one of the girls from the previous night strutted forward, pushing her pointed finger in Nymati's face.

"Who are you to change the rules?" the girl accused, but Nymati looked past her, right through to Drazah who hadn't blinked since Nymati began talking.

"Very well," he said as the rumbling crowd grew tense.

"May I begin?" Nymati smiled, but the tone of her voice had changed. Before she was serious, strong, but now there was eagerness and excitement – malice even.

The first fell so fast many missed it.

Nymati reached forward, grabbing the girl by her clothes and pulling her close. She opened her mouth wide, inhaling as she tore the mana from her opponent. The girl flailed but Nymati held her firm in one hand, draining her dry of mana before dropping her body to the floor.

The crowd exploded in cheers and applause. The air grew suddenly thick as their Sudran bloodlust surged.

Six remained. The girls stood in stunned silence, mouths gaping, as Nymati cracked her fingers. Wisps of mana traced her features as she licked her lips.

"Forfeit now, ladies or surrender your lives," Nymati mocked, brushing raven hair from her face. "I'm not here to take it easy on you."

Leathery wings tore through skin as each of the girls transformed and surrounded Nymati. Two raised to the air, their onyx forms bombing down on Nymati, but she appeared unaffected.

Drazah held still, unable to look away as they closed in. Not the three girls remaining from the previous night, they hung back – *cowards*.

Vicious hands clawed at Nymati in a barrage of failed attempts to hit her. She avoided their attacks with ease, her body flowing seamlessly between their sharpened nails, and slipped between the girl's defences with ethereal grace.

The two girls snapped back as Nymati caught them each by the arm. Bones crumbled beneath her fingers as Nymati clapped her opponents together before her. She heaved them forward into a third girl as she advanced, taking them all out in a single motion.

Only three left now.

They dived forward, racing towards Nymati with incredible speed, but she ignored them, her ruby eyes still set on Drazah through a flurry of flailing fists.

Why wasn't she fighting back? He couldn't understand it, but he couldn't look away.

Then Nymati smirked as she unleashed a wave of energy. Gale force winds tore through the room as her energy surged, a hurricane of raging mana whipping around opponent and spectator alike. Torches retreated as the air grew thin, shadows stretching as Nymati forced her opponents into submission.

The three girls gasped for air. Their eyes spun, desperate as they tried to run, but it was too late. An almighty crack cut through the chaos as the storm suddenly dissipated. The crowds looked to the stage to find only Nymati standing. Silence followed, the entire hall still as they tried to comprehend what just happened.

Drazah still squinted his eyes as Nymati looked around her to see if any of her opponents were able to return to their feet. Her face smug, she placed a hand to her heart and bowed.

The hall erupted as Nymati stood victorious. She had won the tournament and the title of queen. However, none of that mattered as she looked up to her king.

She was his queen and she would do anything for him.

From that moment forth, everything she did would be for him and his people. For now, they were her people too and that was a responsibility she took seriously.

Very, very seriously.

* * *

Child of Devotion

Autumn Year 3651 - 24 BMF

* * *

Change didn't happen all at once.

It was more a series of smaller instances.

Some so small you might have missed them.

But I was always watching...

* * *

Reyla Fenwilt was a quiet child. A daughter of Freya, her green skin warmed with the rising sun, waking her before the rest of her household. She sat in bed and awaited the arrival of her parents, her eyes flicking from their bedroom door to that of her aunt and uncle. The youngest in their household, it was important she behaved and caused no trouble. Besides, Uncle would tell her off if she woke him, and upsetting him ranked among the highest of her things to avoid.

She lived with her parents, aunt and uncle in a two-bedroom grow in Low Town of Ceynas. This left her taking a shabby cot in the main room alongside their kitchen, dining and seating area. Too young to understand the intricacies of poverty and social standing, Reyla saw only the places her family shared each day and it was, for the most part, perfectly pleasant.

Her father was the first to rise, a tall man with wild chestnut hair like hers. Father raked the fireplace clear and threw fire onto fresh logs before setting about breakfast. He worked in the palace kitchen, leaving his hands calloused and his arms thick with muscles as big as Reyla. Compared to her, he was a giant as big as the stone bear statues twinning the city cemetery, but as warm and inviting as the glowing walls of the city temple.

"Up and at 'em." Father banged upon the bedroom doors as he circled the cupboards in search of supplies.

Reyla left her bed and moved to the table. She pushed the wooden chair away and clambered onto the seat.

"How did you sleep, Chicken?" He rubbed his hand over her head and between her pointed ears. "We better get you some breakfast, you'll be going to work with your mother and me today."

Reyla smiled, her hazel eyes filled with youth and potential. It wasn't that she couldn't talk, more that she never found her moment to try. If she did decide to speak, however, she was certain she would want to speak with Father, he was the most fun of their family. She smacked her lips, just to see if anything slipped away from her, when the bedroom door flung open.

"It's going to be one of them days again, I see." Her mother rushed in with a bundle of dirty tunics and undergarments in her hands. "How am I already running late? I'll have to do these tonight."

"Ask Ella."

Mother pulled a face and dropped the clothes into a basket. "It's fine. I'll do it when I get home."

"Suit yourself." He kissed her on the cheek and dealt five plates to the table. A board of bread and a collection of preserve jars soon followed.

Reyla's aunt and uncle joined them as Father passed her a slice of bread slathered in strawberry jam. The sister of her father, her aunt's hair was also chestnut coloured like Reyla's, but it was long and straight with hardly a single strand out of place. Uncle looked like no one, with red hair and eyes the colour of blueberries. Reyla didn't like either of them much and reserved her attention for breakfast, listening while the adults talked.

"Doing much today, El?" Father sat beside Reyla and checked on her progress before eating himself.

"I thought I would wander down to the temple and make a visit to the market." She shirked a purple woollen shawl tighter around her shoulders and gathered it about her chest with measured debility.

"We could do with some vegetables for dinner if you're off down the market. It would save me a trip," said Mother. She still hadn't sat down and continued fussing, making sure everything down to Reyla's bed was straightened before leaving.

Mother was very house-proud and always looked after others. Reyla knew she worked in the palace too but wasn't entirely sure what she did. She never stopped moving, at least not as far as Reyla knew and mess was not allowed in their house.

Her aunt slid her features to Father.

"I'll give you the copper. Don't buy more than you can carry." Reyla didn't need to look to know her mother's eyes were rolling. She didn't understand why Father indulged her aunt and uncle so much.

A sigh rasped from her aunt's lips. "I suppose."

Having neglected her breakfast plate, Mother stole a slice of bread before returning to the bedroom without speaking.

"Was it something I said?" Her aunt placed a hand on her chest in false regret. Even Reyla knew her Aunt didn't mean any of the concern she showed. She was a frail woman who needed support but did nothing for herself or anyone else unless she had to. It was a trait young Reyla found most unappealing.

Mother returned and ushered Reyla into a fresh tunic and leaf-leather shoes. She combed Reyla's hair to the best of her abilities, ensuring she looked acceptable for the day ahead.

"We're ready," she said.

"Me too." Father fastened his belt and pulled a low-hanging satchel over his shoulder. "We'll be back this evening. Have a good day."

Reyla joined Mother in saying goodbye, but her aunt and uncle returned to breakfast without a word. Mother took Reyla by the hand and walked them onto the forest paths between the bungalows of Low Town.

"You're much too lenient with them," Mother barbed to Father. "All I asked was for help with food shopping. You'd think I asked her to paint the house."

"What would you have me do? It's not like we can afford to give her Savulin Tonic."

There were few gardens in Low Town, but the edge of every foot-worn path sprung with grass and wildflowers. Reyla waved her free hand over the tallest blooms, unaware of the conversation around her.

Mother scoffed. "Because that will solve her problems."

Their path met the road as her parents continued bickering and they turned towards the palace. It was much wider and intended for carts and soldiers, but ran right up to the palace gates. A wall of thick hedges marked the edge of the palace grounds, ending where two giant redwood trees were arteformed into the frame of two thick gates.

The gates were open on one side and two guards watched their approach. Reyla eyed the swords upon their belts and the leaf-leather sheaths pressed with floral embellishments with wonderment, but never dared think to touch one herself. They were dangerous, Mother told her. Swords are for boys, said Father. But Reyla thought they were cool.

"Brent. Juna. Putting the little one to work today?"

Her father released a deep-bellied laugh. "Well times are tough, you know. Better to start them young."

It was as if her parents were suddenly different Frey. They forgot their arguments and passed pleasantries as if nothing were ever wrong. Reyla liked them better this way, it was like how they were before her aunt and uncle came to stay with them.

"Don't I know it? Jolie's already got the ovens going so you'd better get going. Let her know I've been stuck out here for us, will you? If we time it right, I can walk her home."

"I can do that for you, lad. You better make your move this time though, you hear me?" Father clapped his hand on the back of the guard and continued past.

Grown and arte-formed over hundreds of years from oak,

cedar and fir, the palace was the biggest building Reyla had ever seen besides the temple. Thick trunks twisted into towers and branches coiled into parapets along arte-formed rooftops with pale Olivewood tiles and walls of sleek unbroken Bulock. It was quiet this time of the morning, but another two guards stood to attention by the doors of brass and oak in the entrance. They didn't go in that way though.

Mother and Father hurried her through a side entrance and down a corridor. To one side, the kitchen door was open and the clattering of pots and bangs of kneaded dough echoed down to meet them. On the other, a door opened to the servants' chamber and a gaggle of young women in white aprons emerged and clustered. Reyla recognised them, but couldn't put a name to any of their faces.

"Off you go, ladies, I'll be with you in a moment," said Mother. She released Reyla's hand to wave them off and turned to Father. "I doubt I'll be leaving the palace today, so I'll come check on you as often as I can."

"Don't worry, we'll be fine. Won't we, Chicken?" He grinned at Reyla and she grinned back.

Mother didn't seem convinced. "Just behave yourselves."

She straightened Reyla's hair and kissed her on the forehead before leaving. Father smirked and pushed on the door to the servants' quarters where Reyla would be spending the next few hours alone, behaving. There was little inside: beds, chairs, a table and a wash basin, so Reyla wasn't sure how she was supposed to misbehave, but she was determined to do her best not to regardless.

Father pulled out a box with wooden toys and scrap paper

inside and emptied them onto the table. He found a few crayons and inspected the wooden horse made from a cork and a few scraps he salvaged from another project. It was crooked and the head drooped, but he used his limited arte skills to smooth the connections and twist the tail.

"Now I've got to go to work, but you'll be just fine in here. If you need anything I'm only across the corridor, okay?"

Reyla bobbed her head. This wasn't the first time she had been left alone and it would certainly not be the last.

"That's my girl." He ruffled her hair, undoing any of her Mother's previous efforts. "I'll come check on you in a bit."

And with that, he was gone and Reyla was alone.

* * *

No one seemed to mind Reyla as she sat in the servants' quarters. Members of the palace staff came and went, often passing their praises on how well-behaved she was as she scribbled on paper, which Reyla found most agreeable.

She reached over the table for the wooden horse and fingered the points and grooves, her thoughts wandering from one childish inclination to the other. First, she thought she would like to try horse riding and wondered how fast they could go. Horses were surely not the fastest creatures on the planet and she got to trying to decide which one was, but was only able to draw on her exposure to the wild animals of Ceynas.

Mother disturbed her thoughts when she entered the chamber with a plate of boiled vegetables and a cup of water.

"Having fun?" Her smile suggested she knew no fun could be had within the confines of this room, but Reyla wasn't going to break her silence to tell her so. "It won't be long until we go home now. I'll come back when I can."

Again her Mother left and Reyla picked at the vegetables with her fingers. She ate the carrots and broccoli, but left the peas, deeming them too fiddly. It wasn't as if anyone was around to make her eat them either.

It was boring sitting in the room all on her own, but Reyla was a good girl and she would do as she was told. It was important to her that she caused no trouble for her parents, at least no more than she could help. There was nothing she could do about her aunt and uncle's determination to find fault with everything she did.

She would be good and do her best, then her parents would fight less. They were so happy when they weren't arguing...

A lady ran in and collected an apron from the bed and returned to the corridor in a whirlwind of motions. She left so fast that the door bounced back from the frame. It creaked inwards, slowly revealing the corridor to Reyla.

"The king wants a pie for dinner," came a voice.

"A pie? But I've already got a stew on," a woman worried.

"Don't ruffle your skirts. I've enough flour to do a pie," Father's voice rang with reason. "Jus' boil it off and stick it inside, he'll never know."

Reyla crept toward the door, peering into the wooden

corridor with caution. Across the way, her father clattered about the kitchen, engrossed in his duties. No one saw her. It was almost an invitation to venture further.

She hesitated. If she was caught she would get into trouble and would be sent to her bed without supper. However, the door at the end of the corridor led to the gardens where a world of adventure and discovery called to her.

It would only be misbehaving if she got caught. Who would even know she had gone? If she were really fast, and only peeked through the door a little, no one would ever know she left her room at all.

Reyla checked up and down the corridor once more and waited for Father to delve deeper into the kitchen. Confident the coast was clear, she slipped through and skipped out the back of the palace.

Butterflies filled Reyla's stomach as the door snapped shut behind her. The sun crisped the air and the warm breeze flared the bottom of Reyla's tunic, flowing over the gardens to the paddocks and training grounds beyond.

The palace gardens bloomed with lilies, the beds following a path to the pond where they would feed the fish some days. There were benches elsewhere in the gardens, but the ones near the pond were the best. Or so Reyla thought, and in an instant, her plans of returning to her room were forgotten.

Reyla roamed the garden path to the end where the exterior hedges stopped and opened into paddocks. She followed along the fence to the barracks, her hand tapping the poles as she passed them. The horses in the paddocks were Whisps, the rare breed of horses used only by the royal family, with soft pistachio green coats and thick manes of waving moss-green. They didn't seem to notice her and remained effortlessly gracious and beautiful even in their neglect.

Reyla's ears twitched as she neared the mess hall, catching her next adventure.

Steel clanged from the sparring pit as she rounded into the training yards, a small gathering of Frey blocking her view. She hesitated, having been told to stay away from the barracks by her parents many times before, but curiosity called her closer.

It wasn't misbehaving if no one saw her. If she was careful and hugged the wall, no one would even know she was there.

"Pudra attack with axe and fist, but the Estra fight with sword and spear." A Frey with steel armour and a white cloak kicked a crate to the centre of the sparring pit and jumped upon it, a long spear in his hands. "With their horse bodies, they'll be coming down on you from above. Flaxel. Valren. Show us how you'd deal with them."

Two men stepped forward. They wore leaf-leather armour and green capes with short swords and round shields on their arms. One had a face as long and narrow as the Whisps Reyla passed earlier, he perpetuated the resemblance further by tying his hair into an even longer ponytail, the colour washed with greys and silvers despite his youth. The other was far more handsome and spry, his narrow features pointed and a shock of white-blonde hair resting about a sharp smirk which piqued Reyla's interest.

She had never seen them before. Who were they?

Reyla moved closer, peering between the guards to see the action.

The Frey in the white cape was far uglier than she expected from further away. It looked like a crow pinched a giant notch from his nose and a purple scar crossed his cheek where healers used artes to seal some grievous injury. By Reyla's reckoning, he was the oldest man in the whole of the training yards. Except for the depot keeper, she heard he was even older than the palace.

"Take your best shot lads. Remember, the Estra won't be standing still neither."

The horse-faced Frey took a few arbitrary swings with his sword, dipping back as if to test his opponent's reach. He held back, allowing the handsome guard to move in - who bowed and dodged but was only ever able to defend with his shield.

"Come on, is that the best you've got?" The notch-nosed man teased and swung his spear across the rear of the horse-faced guard. "Again."

The other Frey grit his teeth, his sword hilt tightened into his waist as he rushed forward. Pointing his blade at the notched-nosed man, he lunged from behind, hoping to find an opening, but the spear flicked to meet him. It deflected the sword and continued its arc, forcing the guards to the sides.

"Again."

This time the two guards separated. They circled the man on the crate, a secret conversation passing between them. Without ever speaking a word, they formed their plan and set it in motion. It was like magic.

Reyla's thoughts emptied, entirely captivated as they readied their swords and pressed the offensive. Horse-face ran in first, blocking as the spear spun to meet him. As metal rung through the yard, the roguish one thought to rear their opponent but caught metal with his face and ducked away. The notched-nosed man used both ends of his spear to attack, the thunk of wood and steel upon their helms setting the two guards dizzy.

They staggered forward, barely holding their balance when the spear swung again. It caught them each round the ear and Reyla's heart dropped to the ground with the pair of them. The guardsmen cheered in a riotous mixture of insults and support.

Laughing, the guard before Reyla turned and caught her eye. "Hey, kid!"

Reyla started and spun on her heel. They saw her!

With her heart in her mouth, she ran as fast as her legs could carry her. Between the barracks and the mess hall. Along the paddocks. Back into the palace gardens.

If she ran fast enough, no one would know it was her.

No one could tell her parents what she had done.

Reyla gasped for breath and slowed within the safety of the lilies. Out of sight, out of mind, she now found herself by the pond in the centre of the gardens, her thoughts now filled with fish and frogs and lily pads.

It was Reyla's favourite place in the palace. There were so many different plants and animals, there would be something new for her to discover every time she visited.

Searching for her latest discovery, Reyla found she was not the only one enjoying the pond that day. She straightened, uncertain as she stared at the woman on the bench.

The woman was Frey, and possibly the most beautiful woman Reyla had ever seen. Waves of glossy moss-green hair flowed beyond her shoulders, and she had eyes like glistening emeralds set in a bed of porcelain-green skin so perfect it seemed to glow like The Life Tree. She smiled, plump juniper lips peaking with kindness.

"Having an adventure are we?"

Reyla's cheeks burned. Adults hardly ever addressed her directly and never ones as ethereal as the woman on the bench.

"Come closer, child. It's all right."

Reyla edged closer. Mother said never to talk to strangers, but she recognised this lady from the painting in the hall and she seemed so pleasant. Much more pleasant than her aunt and uncle, so she couldn't be all that bad. Could she?

Reyla investigated the woman further. She held something in her arms forcing Reyla onto her toes to get a better look. It was swaddled within a silk wrap and the woman bobbed it in her arms in a repetitive motion.

"She's sleeping right now, but you can look if you're quiet."

Reyla nodded her head and held her silence. The silk shuffled, revealing a soft blush set over rounded cheeks and wisps of mossy-green baby hairs.

"This is Princess Arafrey. She will be your queen one day."

Reyla marvelled at the precious bundle, a strange sense of purpose upon her heart. She didn't understand the feeling, but she understood this child was important.

"I hope one day you and Ara can become friends. Would

you like that?"

Reyla bobbed her head and the baby babbled.

"I'm sure she would like that too." The woman's smile radiated with the warmth of a thousand hugs. Reyla didn't care what it was, if she asked it of her, Reyla would surely do it just to see her smile again. "My daughter will have much to endure when she is older. I should feel much better knowing my daughter has friends like you to watch out for her."

Reyla couldn't take her eyes off the tiny princess. Her chest filled with something which was both warm and heavy around her heart. Something far beyond her juvenile comprehension and yet somehow she understood.

Overcome with an overwhelming desire to protect something so precious, Reyla's mouth opened to declare her intentions when-

"Reyla! There you are." Mother ran at Reyla, her face red.

Reyla's eyes flung wide, her crimes apparent. She shrunk in on herself, certain a heavy scolding lay in her future as Mother grabbed her by the hand.

"I'm so sorry, Your Highness. She wondered off and-"

"There's no need to apologize, Juna. Reyla's a delightful child. It's better she comes to me than one with ill intentions."

Mother bowed, she wouldn't even look at Reyla. "Of course, Your Highness. You're much too kind and generous as always."

Reyla's shoulder ached as Mother stomped them back to the palace, her eyes upon the baby who would one day be her queen.

"You're in so much trouble, young lady," her Mother scolded as the door closed, but Reyla didn't care. "You'll be going straight to your bed when you get home."

* * *

Seeds of Light

Spring Year 3652 – 23 BMF

* * *

Princess Elsafrey cradled her daughter, rocking the arte-formed chair gently as she fed. The long flowing lengths of her moss-green hair rested over the shoulders of her nightgown, the soft linen like silvery silk.

The sun crept in through the curtains, lighting their bedroom in a soft umber glow. Galafrey still slept, the green points of his ears poking from a mess of bedsheets and brown, oaken hair. He had never been a morning person and she allowed him to rest, enjoying the quiet moment with her daughter.

Arafrey was a few months old but was smaller than Elsafrey would hope. If she were advising a patient in the temple, she would tell them not to worry while their child continued to eat, yet still, she felt her failings like a gut punch. How was she supposed to heal their people when she couldn't even raise her own child properly?

A knock interrupted her thoughts and Juna entered. Her handmaid was always the first in each morning despite having a child of her own. Juna had her hair pulled up into a tight vertical roll this morning, a sure sign of her pressing workload for the day.

"Good morning, Princess. Your Highness." She drew the curtains and gathered garments from the wardrobes. "His Grace has already gone down to the dining hall for breakfast and hopes for you to join him."

Galafrey grumbled, moaned, and folded the duvet away from him. He rolled his feet over the side of the mattress and pushed himself upright, his naked torso a pistachio-green delight in the eyes of his princess. Juna helped pass a thin tunic over his head and held a robe to put his arms inside.

Elsafrey finished nursing and passed young Arafrey to the cot. "If you would like, I could make an excuse for you on my way to the temple."

Galafrey wrapped his hands around her middle and kissed her cheek. "But what's the point of staying in our room all day, if you'll leave me alone."

Elsafrey smiled and chose not to point out she would be leaving their daughter at home while she tended the temple. She kissed his cheek and asked Juna to watch Arafrey while they attended breakfast.

* * *

King Idofrey and High Priestess Yarafrey were already seated among mounds of toast, fruit and condiments when they arrived.

Elsafrey passed idle pleasantries as she took a seat, but received no more than incoherent grunts and nods from her in-laws. She tried to remind herself of the trouble Galafrey had getting out of bed each morning, but was unable to find an excuse for them the rest of the time. They were possibly the only people on the planet Elsafrey couldn't find a single positive thing to say about, and she was already counting the days to their retirement and the day they moved from the palace.

King Idofrey sat at the head of their table, reading his notices over a cup of tea. A crown of solid gold wrapped around his head, long straights of greyed-oaken hair framing the harsh lines of his face.

"We've been sent an invitation to Prince Drazah's wedding."

"Oh?" Yarafrey's nose lifted as she processed the information. "We shall have to send something. I don't fancy traipsing across the desert at any time of the year."

"Quite right," Idofrey nodded. "We're hardly familiar with their customs either. I dread to think what the Sudra do for a wedding. One minute they're civilized and the next they're charming and fornicating. It's most uncultured."

Elsafrey didn't agree with his summation but breakfast was not the time to raise an argument with her king and father-in-law. "Perhaps we would do well to learn more of their customs if we are to work together in the future. How soon is it? Galafrey and I could go if you wish?"

"And take Ara with you to Sudra?" Yarafrey's disapproval was paramount.

"No, of course not," Elsafrey panicked.

"You would leave her at home? Is she ready to be away from her mother?"

Elsafrey flustered, unable to find the correct answer for the situation.

"I think it's worth considering." Galafrey placed his hand on her knee beneath the table, the strong monotone of his voice working to ease her frustrations. "Our visit to Pudron certainly proved fruitful. Befriending our neighbours and strengthening our position in Alamantra is the least we can do for our kingdom."

Idofrey shared a look with Yarafrey, "If that is how you wish to spend your time, it's not for me to tell you which parties to attend."

Elsafrey pressed her tongue between her teeth for fear she may say something she could not take back. Monarch or not, the great King Idofrey looked down upon the rest of Alamantra and she could never forgive him for it. Many Frey followed his example and it encouraged the unrest and bias engrained within their people. Not that Yarafrey was any better, but she was cruel and callous in her own ways.

Galafrey reached for the notice and read the contents for himself. "We wouldn't have to set off for a few months yet. Will you be ready to travel by then?"

The softness within the monotones of his concern were among the many reasons Elsafrey loved him. They were so gentle few could even hear them, but to Elsafrey, they were a sonnet spoken only for her.

"Maybe we should think on it," she conceded, if only to avoid further argument, "If suitable arrangements can be made, I would love to attend. I shall have to give some thought to a wedding gift. I've no idea what Sudra consider a gift."

"A bloody animal carcass probably," jibed Idofrey. Yarafrey's top lip lifted to expose her teeth as they jeered together. "What was it they sent for our wedding? Some stone cat?"

It was a totem carved and chiselled in the likeness of a bear, but Elsafrey didn't correct him. Normally, the Sudra would carve lions, elephants and other native animals into their effigies in order to manifest spirits of strength and fortune, but the bear was unique. It was an Urous Bear, native to Freya, yet the tribute was lost on their mighty king and queen.

Elsafrey set her utensils aside and wiped her mouth. "If you'll excuse me, I would like to pray before work today."

The king and queen mumbled something, but Elsafrey was as good at ignoring them as she was at holding her tongue. She leaned in and kissed Galafrey on the cheek.

"I'll be back this afternoon."

* * *

It was still quiet when Elsafrey arrived in the city temple.

The light of The Life Tree warmed the temple courtyard as she entered, its roots forming the walls and wrapping around into the temple itself. It grew far beyond the forest canopy, glowing with the mystic blue hue of the Manastream circling their planet. The pews were empty as she crossed to the front of the courtyard where a pool of water collected. Its surface hummed with the mana collected on its way down the ancient tree and it lit Elsafrey's features as she knelt to pray.

Clasping her hands together, Elsafrey prayed for the health and well-being of her people and the happiness of those she loved. She prayed for wisdom and strength, for she could never have too much, and thanked the Gods for her patience, for it was truly tested by her king and queen. Finally, Elsafrey prayed for the future of Prince Drazah and his wife-to-be, and resolved to find them the perfect gift.

Someone whispered in Elsafrey's ear, forcing her to stand. She spun, expecting to see someone there, but there was nothing.

Elsafrey clutched her hands to her chest, the beat of her heart pounding behind them. Her emerald eyes darted from the pews to the temple corridor and along the smooth spans of tree back to her feet. There was nothing.

Shaking her head, Elsafrey returned to the temple building and went in search of Sister Alma.

While the courtyard was used for service and prayers, the temple building was made up of wards and examination rooms to tend to the health of the local citizens. Elsafrey found Sister Alma in a ward on the second floor, tending patients. She wore a cream robe wrapped with an apron and habit which hid her hair and ears, the uniform of the temple aides.

"Good morning, Princess." Alma smiled. Elsafrey considered her such a pleasant woman with a sunny disposition, but Sister Alma was more dedicated to their work than most anyone in the temple.

"Where shall I start?"

"I've just these beds to change then we can start downstairs." Sister Alma pointed to the recently vacated beds across the ward.

Elsafrey's cheer depressed. "What happened to Mr Linbalm? I thought he was getting better."

"We thought so too. I knew we should've tried bellum root first." Alma whipped a sheet over the bed in an effort to clear her fury.

Elsafrey was there when Yarafrey ordered the treatment for Mr Linbalm. He was a sickly old man who was struck with a persistent fever. Bellum root would have been a gentler way to ease the fever slowly, yet their high priestess insisted they use Bargot and Savulin Tonic so their patient could be back on his feet by morning. It was an outdated and dangerous treatment. They tried to speak up but were unable to sway Yarafrey in any way, much to their patient's detriment.

With the beds changed, Elsafrey followed Sister Alma and continued their rounds. They changed bandages and checked temperatures. They fetched drinks and extra pillows. They did all they could for their patients within the constraints of Yarafrey's law, and when they were done, they stopped in the corridor to rest on the floor.

"I don't know how you put up with her." Sister Alma sighed, her voice low, ever aware of the many patients around them.

"Nor I sometimes." Elsafrey would never speak an ill word of anyone, but she allowed herself a moment to think some of Yarafrey. "I think it's not her fault though. Not fully. She cannot see how dangerous clinging to the old ways can be, especially when one holds the life of another in their hands."

Sister Alma's head bobbed and she smiled. "Let's just thank the Gods you will be high priestess soon."

"Hmmm." Elsafrey was more than ready to become high priestess. She worked, trained and studied alongside some of the greatest healers and teachers in the whole of Freya since becoming princess. Her preparations for it began long before that, however, back when her father conspired with Idofrey to introduce young Elsa to the eligible Prince Galafrey as often as possible.

A shiver ran down Elsafrey's spine as the whispers returned. She whipped her head back over her shoulder, but again there was nothing there.

"Princess?"

Elsafrey stared along the corridor, her brows knitted. There was hardly any corridor left behind them. A single ward door lay on one side and a window the other, and in the middle lay the door to the catacombs.

"Did you hear that?"

"Hear wha-?"

"Shush, shush."

Elsafrey leaned further down the corridor and the whispers returned.

"Can't you hear that?"

Alma shook her head, but Elsafrey was already rising to her feet. She held her breath, her head tilting as she tried to direct her ears towards the sounds. They were quiet now, soft like spring showers on the palace walls. Elsafrey could not discern them and opened the old door in hopes of hearing more, but the only thing leaving the catacombs was the stale air from deep underground.

"Do you think there's someone in the catacombs?"

Elsafrey released her breath, as disappointed as she was frustrated. "There's only one way to find out."

"Should I go get a guard? It could be dangerous."

"And tell them what?" Elsafrey tied her hair back into a messy knot above her pointed ears. "Sister, you can stay here if you wish, but I'm going in."

"No, I'm coming." Sister Alma wasn't pleased as she stepped in beside her. "His Highness would send me to Old Wood as a traitor if anything happened and I left you."

Elsafrey chuckled. "Come now, what's the worst that can happen to us down there? We both know the scariest things in Freya reside in the palace."

* * *

The catacombs spanned as far and as deep as the roots of The Life Tree. Here the Frey kings and queens of ages past rested among placards and trinkets left in tribute by those who followed.

There was no need for lights as the roots of The Life Tree filled the soil walls with glowing patterns. The gentle blue glow allowed them safe passage as Elsafrey ventured further.

Elsafrey could no longer hear the whispers, yet still, something called her further inside.

"Elsa, what are you doing? There's no one here."

She continued walking, unable to stop herself. "I- I can't

explain it. There's this pull in my chest. It draws me here."

Elsafrey held her hand before her and activated her artes. Mana rushed through her body to her hand, where it collected and glowed white. The pull grew stronger, guiding her by the hand deeper into the catacombs. It drew her deeper and deeper into the bowels of The Life Tree, past the tombs of long forgotten kings and queens to an area she did not know existed.

"Maybe we should turn back. There's no one here."

"I'm not so sure." Elsafrey held her artes over the wall ahead of her. "There's something strange about this place."

"I don't see how. It's all mud and soil and roots, just like the rest of this place."

Elsafrey wet her lips, her concentration doubling. She was certain she heard something, but the evidence spoke to the contrary. Was she losing her mind? Or was she missing something?

The whispers returned as Elsafrey ran her artes over the roots of The Life Tree, and Alma yelped. "What was that?"

"Directions."

"Directions where?"

Elsafrey smirked. "I don't know. Let's find out."

The whispers grew in number and speed, directing Elsafrey further along the tunnel. They were too fast and too many to hear even a single word, but their excitement, their urgency wrapped Elsafrey's body and carried her on. As a woman possessed, she allowed it to take her, the glow of her artes running over the wall until reaching a knot in the roots.

Elsafrey's body jolted as the knot connected with her palm. A bright light seemed to fuse her artes to the tree, but Elsafrey was unable to release them. She cried out in pain, the whispers screaming alongside her as the mana was torn from her body.

A sudden burst of power flung Elsafrey back against the catacomb wall. The light was sucked from the roots of The Life Tree, plunging them into darkness, all except for a single point. The knot. It was no longer a knot in a root though, instead a thick green stem grew from its core.

Elsafrey coughed and staggered to her feet. A flower budded before her eyes, shining with mana through the dust and debris filling the air. The bud grew to the size of a melon and white petals pushed through the centre. They multiplied and grew like an egg, then unfurled around a bed of black florets to reveal a strange face like a sunflower.

It was beautiful and unlike any flower Elsafrey had ever seen, yet somehow, she knew what to do.

Elsafrey activated her artes over the flower and called to the seeds inside. It was a delicate process, willing the flower to give up its bounty of its own accord, but a process she was well versed in.

The white sunflower shuddered and a single seed the size of a strawberry appeared in the middle. It fell into Elsafrey's hands, the surface black and rough, and then the sunflower petals wilted. The flower died and light returned to the catacombs as it crumbled into dust and vanished.

Sister Alma shuffled over to take a closer look. "Is this what we were looking for?"

"A seed?" It was as much a question as it was a statement.

"From The Life Tree?"

"Do you think it will grow another Life Tree?"

Elsafrey activated her artes, allowing her to look deeper into the composition of the seed. It was so strange and made from things she held no name for. "No, I don't think it will."

"Then what?"

Elsafrey giggled, "So impatient, Sister. I think we're supposed to plant it and see for ourselves."

* * *

Elsafrey returned to the temple with Sister Alma and helped serve lunch to their patients before leaving for the palace.

Men gathered in the entrance hall as she entered, no doubt waiting to see King Idofrey. They each bowed upon noticing her, their flowing robes and long hair suggesting they were noble Frey. Elsafrey dipped her head as much as was required of her and continued past, down the corridor to the greenhouse.

Grown at the back of the palace, the greenhouse arced down from between the first and second floor. It had windows made from leaf epidermis, stretched and hardened until clear enough to refract the sunlight and warm the plants inside. Sleeping vines hung from baskets on the rafters and wooden racks housed pots of soil hoping to sprout.

Elsafrey lifted an empty plant pot onto the workbench and pulled mulch and soil from the bags below. She padded the bottom of the pot with pebbles and built a nest to bury the white sunflower seed in. Once it was covered, Elsafrey sprinkled water over the surface and stroked the side of the pot as if it were a cat.

With great thought to the weather, season and creation of the white sunflower, Elsafrey chose to leave the pot on the workbench. Set within the shadow of the hanging baskets, the workbench caught its fair share of sun, but not so much as to overheat anyone working there in summer. It should, she hoped, provide a more neutral environment for the seed to grow, at least until she discovered its preferences.

Elsafrey adjusted the pot and pet it once more.

"Grow well, little one. I'll be back to water you tomorrow."

* * *

Elsafrey planned to visit the temple and tend to her duties before returning to the greenhouse the next day. However, her plans were quickly abandoned when Juna rushed to the bedroom to fetch her.

"Samia's in a real fluster, My Lady. He says you've been experimenting in the greenhouse again. You'd better get down there."

Elsafrey knew the groundskeeper was especially precious with the greenhouse and didn't like her leaving things there, so she left for the greenhouse expecting a scolding. What she received upon arriving, however, was nothing of the sort.

"My Lady!" Samia gaped from the centre of the greenhouse,

his eyes like saucers. "I came in this morning and watched as the whole nursery budded and bloomed. I've never seen anything so magical."

Every plant, on every shelf, was in full bloom. Vines ran greener than newborn sproutlings and their leaves gleamed with vibrancy. The entire greenhouse appeared to have grown overnight alongside the white sunflower now sitting in a pot on the workbench.

Elsafrey inspected the white sunflower more closely. It wasn't as big as the one from the catacombs but it smelt just as sweet and the petals were white as snow. She collected a seed tray from the workbench and held it beneath the flower as she activated her artes over the shiny black florets at its centre.

Sparks of electricity rose through Elsafrey's body, her artes touching upon seed after seed after seed. She extended her control over the flower, the glow of her mana flicking shadows around the greenhouse. Then, the white petals shimmied and dozens of tiny black seeds fell from its core to the tray.

Elsafrey released her artes, her mouth open wordlessly as she stared in awe at the bounty before her.

"My- My Lady, what is this plant?"

"I don't know." Elsafrey smiled. "But I'm going to find out."

* * *

Over the coming months, Princess Elsafrey continued to breed the white sunflowers and track their progress.

Despite a short gestation period, they appeared to have a lifecycle spanning several weeks when kept in groups. However, once separated from the others this reduced significantly. Each day she could harvest a trove of seeds to save for later experiments, but struggled to find an application for the flowers themselves.

As far as Elsafrey could tell, the white sunflowers held no mana or special qualities, yet they seemed to have an encouraging effect on the other plants stored in the greenhouse. Further experimentation, involving moving the white sunflowers into larger pots and sitting them in different points of the palace gardens, proved the phenomenon was not restricted to the greenhouse and helped judge the reach of each flower with the radius of plants blooming around them. From there she tested it on lawns and fields, vegetable plots and vineyards, each experiment more spectacular than the last.

Under Elsafrey's care, Ceynas flourished from Low Town to The Life Tree. It was all incredibly rewarding work, but not, it appeared, enough to sway the affections of her king and queen.

"Do you intend on running the sermon tomorrow, or will you be playing with your flowers again, Elsa?" Yarafrey sneered over her dinner plate.

Elsafrey chewed her food longer than was necessary. Merely dropping the suffix from her name was meant as an insult, but it was one Elsafrey was destined to suffer in silence. "Unless you wish me somewhere else. I had my aide ready my robes though."

Elsafrey didn't bother sharing names with Idofrey or Yarafrey as they were sure to not know, or rather not care, what the names of their staff were. It was a trait her dear husband sadly adopted, but it was more poor memory than ill manners which caused him to forget.

"You could give her a little more credit than that, Mother." The timbre of Galafrey's voice remained steady, but it was not often he spoke up against his parents. "Elsa's replenished the crop fields from last year with her flowers. We're set to quadruple our yield."

Yarafrey's lips tightened, a thick vein throbbing by her temple. "Yes, well, I was merely making sure her duties are not being neglected. We need to ensure preparations are made if you're still intent on going to Sudra."

"We are," Galafrey asserted.

"I'd like to gift the newlyweds a batch of white sunflower seeds," said Elsafrey. "I would be interested to see how they fare in the desert."

Galafrey smiled, a rarity for him, but it was turned upside-down as the Frey King choked on his potatoes.

"You want to share something The Life Tree gifted to you with the Sudra?" Idofrey wheezed and wiped his hand over his face. "What would Sudra do with your flowers?"

"Grow them, I should hope, and use them to grow crops to feed their people."

"No." Idofrey's face hung with a grim ire, his eyes hollow. His word final.

* * *

Elsafrey left the table soon after. She thought to ease her irritation by entertaining her daughter, but Arafrey was already tired when she arrived in their room to claim her and she was put promptly to bed. It was becoming an all too regular occurrence, but Elsafrey consoled herself with the fact her daughter was unlikely to miss her while they visited Sudra.

A sigh rasped from Elsafrey's lips as she watched over the light of her life. It was a sigh of exhaustion and sorrow, anger and hurt. She was ashamed of her king and his selfish ways. She condemned her high priestess for her inability to listen. But more than anything she was disappointed in herself for believing they could be anything more.

Galafrey pressed in beside her, smiling in a way only Elsafrey could see.

"You forgot this." Galafrey continued watching their daughter sleeping as he offered a small arte-formed box.

Elsafrey scrunched her face. The wood was carved with a golden inlay of flowers and the brass hinges were polished so bright they could be mistaken for gold. It was beautiful, but she did not recognise it.

"Go on." Galafrey shook the box without looking.

Accepting the box with a mix of curiosity and suspicion, Elsafrey pushed the lid open. Inside, a trove of black seeds sat on a bed of green satin.

"The seeds! But what about-?"

"My father won't even know they're gone." Galafrey wrapped his arm around her shoulder and kissed the top of her head. "Besides, some discoveries are not ours to keep."

"Your father will be furious if he finds out." Elsafrey leant her head against his shoulder.

"Then let him be furious," said Galafrey, more a king worthy of her devotion in that moment than he ever was. "This was your gift. You get to decide who you share it with, not him."

"Then I shall sow white sunflowers from Pudron to Ruglor," Elsafrey declared, the quiet act of defiance easing the hurts of a thousand verbal jabs. "Although, we may have to come up with a better name for them."

Galafrey took a moment to breathe and give it some thought. "What about Elpidanthus Majorium?"

"What?" Elsafrey laughed. "No one's going to remember that."

"Well, then call them Moon Flowers and have done with it. Either way, they will make the perfect gift to symbolise our new friendship."

Galafrey rubbed her arm in quiet support as they pressed their heads together, neither fully aware of all they accomplished that day.

* * *

I sat back and returned my scope to The Life Tree.

Its view continued down, deep within the bowels of The Life Tree and beyond the knot which sprouted the newly named Moon Flower. There a ripple ran across the surface of a glowing pool of water.

Shining among the muck and flowers and roots, the water shifted and waited, contented in its nature.

The first trial was underway.

* * *

Season of the Witch

Spring Year 3652 - 23BMF

* * *

Fear not the wolf in sheep's clothing,

For it is the shepherd who carries a knife…

* * *

The afternoon sun beamed through a cloudless sky on the Sudran city of Halda as Prince Drazah climbed the rear stairs cut into the palace plateau. Dressed in only a loose beige tunic, which hung to his knees, and leather sandals, his lean muscles glistened with sweat from a hard day of training. His tail flicked carelessly behind him, a charcoal black to match the rest of his skin.

Drazah crested the stairs to the plateau, the palace before him. While the front of the palace was a solid face of painted sandstone spanning three floors, the rear stepped away from the balcony of the royal suite on the top floor. The rooftops were barren, just walls of sandstone and open wooden barrels left there with the dim hope of rainfall. It was where he lived, but the young prince was unsure how much it was his home at that moment.

The plateau itself was busy with staff offloading supplies from the lift. A beautiful unbroken view of Sudra lay before them, yet no one wished to linger to admire it. The charred corpses of burnt witches dangled from spikes stuck into the sides of the rock, and the smell of rotting flesh hung over the palace in the still desert air. Crows circled overhead in a swarm. Having already picked the carcasses clean of eyes and soft flesh, they seldom landed but continued to defecate over anyone unlucky enough to be outside.

Two ladies covered their hair as they left the palace and crossed the plateau towards Drazah. He recognised them from his mother's staff but wasn't acquainted with them well enough to remember their names.

"Ladies." He dipped his head and grinned, the flash of his sharpened fangs more effective than any charm.

"Your Highness." They curtseyed and giggled as they walked away.

Drazah always made sure to stay on the good side of his mother's staff. Not that he was interested in them any, in fact, he considered them all equally meddlesome, but he played to their affections to keep his name from their lips. They were indentured to his mother and would think little of betraying him to her.

He continued inside, cutting through the first-floor rooftop to avoid passing anyone in the corridors. Drazah now shared a room with his paramour on the first floor, a suite of sorts with a lounging area and furnishings enough to create their own space within the palace. It was dark when he entered though. The shutters were closed and the only light came from flickering candles on the table.

A long plume of smoke engulfed the candlelight, the flames swirling and trailing into the air. Drazah gained inches. Nymati, his love, his paramour, his queen and Goddess, sat among the throws and pillows of the lounger, a lit cigarette held to her ebony lips.

"You're back!"

Drazah lifted Nymati into his arms, tiny as she was in his giant's grasp. Thin glittering fabric and long raven hair flowed as he spun and pressed his lips against hers. He didn't care if all he could taste was smoke. His queen was home, and nothing could feel better.

"How was your family?" Nymati had been away a few weeks.

"I'm afraid my aunt succumbed to her illness before I arrived. My uncle decided to return south to be with his own family, so we mostly just made arrangements together."

"I'm sorry. That's terrible." Drazah returned Nymati to the floor and opened a window. He didn't like her smoking inside but wouldn't press the matter when her mood ran sour.

"If only that were the most of my troubles. I was shocked to discover the extent of our witch problems. I thought it was just here in Halda, but there were witches burning in every village we entered."

She returned to her pile of soft furnishings and rummaged through the layers for her cigarette tin. Nymati found the silver tin and placed a hand-rolled cigarette to her ebony lips. Striking a match against the tin, she held the flickering flame to the end and inhaled with her frustrations.

"There were more on the way back too. It's most distressing. I didn't marry you to spend my regency burning our citizens, my love."

Drazah sighed and ran a hand through burnt-umber hair. "What would you have me do when not even the threat of death by pyre is enough to dissuade them?"

Nymati drew on her cigarette with a long, thoughtful pause. She watched him, her eyes blood red in the darkness, and exhaled. "Perhaps we need to consider a different approach."

"You speak as if it's my decision, yet I am not the king. All I do is sweat it out in the training yards all day."

"But you will be king someday and will have to make these decisions for yourself. Stop thinking like a prince, and think like the king you are to me. You already know what you would do about these witches if you were king today."

"Do I?" Drazah shook his head. Nymati always seemed to have more faith in him than Drazah did. "These witches are worse than a lizard infestation and all we seem to be doing is chopping off their tails to let them return."

"No, I think they're a little more organised than lizards." An array of golden bracelets jingled as Nymati leant over to smush the end of her cigarette into the bronze ashtray. "They're more like hornets or ants."

Drazah snorted. "Well, the only way to remove a nest is to capture their queen."

Drazah's brow furrowed and his mouth hung open, ready to bite upon the answer he sought. He was only joking, but was that the answer? Was it that simple? Were they simply reprimanding people too far down on the food chain?

Nymati's lips peeked knowingly and Drazah descended upon her. His hands grasped every curve and swerve of her form, wrapping their bodies together among the cushions.

"My queen, your cunning never ceases to amaze me."

He breathed in her sweet aroma, kissed the slate-coloured

skin of her breast and buried his head within the warmth of her bosom. Warm hands pressed his skin, a soft glow about Nymati's hands as she activated her charm. Drazah welcomed it, craved it.

"The stories say the witches roam in covens." Nymati stroked his hair, her charm flowing as she whispered. It swept through his senses, easing, invigorating, calling him to attention. "We have no way to tell who runs them."

"You call them witches as if they are Gods, but they are just Sudra. And Sudra can be bought or charmed." He lifted his head from her breast, his thoughts sparking from one plan to the next. "We will need people we can trust."

"You have your men."

"No, we need ones people won't miss, to avoid raising suspicions. No one must know of our plans."

A shiver clenched his stomach as Nymati ran her nail along his neck to the point of his ear and back down again. He wanted her to feed on him. It had been so long, she was surely starved, but he liked that she made him wait. She opened her mouth to tease him, his anticipation at what was to come throbbing through his tunic against her.

"Then we should raise our own army." Nymati cupped his face, the warmth of her charm lingering even after she released her artes. She stroked his cheek. "A secret army beholden to only you and I, tasked to seek out the leaders of these covens who terrorise our kingdom."

"A secret army," Drazah repeated, their plans laying down before them. It seemed so simple. Could they do it? Could they take down the covens from the top?

Nymati wet her lips and pulled his head up to hers. She activated her artes, her charm working to prepare his body.

"There's nothing we can't do together, my king."

He believed it to be true. He could do anything with his queen by his side.

Drazah's eyes rolled back as Nymati fed upon him. Pure energy from deep within his mana core rose like a geyser, bursting from his lips into hers in an explosion of pure euphoria. They were one in that moment, joined core to core through their parabond. Ecstasy curled his toes as she sipped upon his strength - and he could wait no longer.

Drazah pulled away, his charcoal skin glowing like the moon against a night sky as he threw off his tunic. He presented his body to her as a tribute of gleaming muscles and stiff readiness.

"For you, my queen, I would raise a thousand armies."

* * *

And so, they raised their army. At least, as much of an army as you could call ten Sudra. They sent men and women, whores and sell-swords, into Halda with the promise of untold riches to anyone who returned to them with a name.

Drazah was all but certain their army would return with nothing, but it pleased Nymati that he made the effort. And she was always so grateful. However, it was only a few days after they began their venture that Nymati came to him with word.

"They're certain?"

"She said he has a room hidden behind the bookcase in the study. They had her stand in the middle of a glowing circle and pledge her fealty to the coven."

"Was she injured?"

"The bastards marked her with a rune." Nymati shook her head as she hissed. "Master Barrick thinks he knows a way to remove it, but we cannot allow them to continue going around marking our people. They must be stopped at all costs."

"And they will be."

Drazah held Nymati to his chest. She cared for their people as much as he did and felt their hurt as if it were her own.

"I'll see to it."

* * *

Drazah left Nymati for the barracks.

A gold khopesh swung from his waist belt as Drazah assembled his men, a company of twenty Sudra clad in leathers and equipped with spears, short swords and daggers. He ordered them to ready two carts and horses and had one loaded with firewood and a stake. The men fell in line before him, awaiting their orders.

Sabutok, his lieutenant, cocked his brow over the kindling. "A bit much, don't you think?"

"We want them to know we're serious, don't we?"

Sabutok grinned, the blazing sun bouncing from his naked head between his horns. He had been bald as long as Drazah could remember him, but was only a few years his senior. The pair were often evenly matched, but had yet to go all out when sparring. Drazah imagined Sabutok held a transformation as impressive as his own, but it was not something one showed unless fighting to the death.

Drazah mounted a brown stallion and guided their party through the narrow sand-beaten streets of Halda. Sabutok rode beside him, his reins pulled just enough to give Drazah the respectable lead. They made a show of it, the braying of horses and the beat of feet on the sand. The trundle of the cartwheels and the promise of the pyre carried inside. The common folk bowed their heads and dipped back into buildings, each quietly praying the convoy would pass them by.

Their destination was an estate just east of the city limits. A two-storey manse with a large wall of grey stones wrapping around a bleak yellowed garden. It belonged to Kaiser Nurzi Ram, a man of high esteem in his father's court. There were ten Kaiser Lords in Halda, each holding dominion over various boroughs of the city, and Kaiser Ram ran the eastern quarter on this side of the Ballish. He was an imposing man of many years. From the burial grounds to the palace plateau, nothing happened without him knowing.

Drazah drew his breath as he knocked upon the solid door and held it in hopes of retaining his height. They would only get one chance to prove his guilt. It was down to him to make it count.

It was Kaiser Ram who answered the door, causing Drazah to falter. He expected the Kaiser to have at least one member of staff and found it suspicious from the offset.

"Prince Drazah? To what do I owe the pleasure?" Kaiser Ram spoke with a gravelly voice to match his demeanour. Grey whiskers covered his cheeks and neck, which met with wild hair which flamed with white streaks above his horns.

"Sorry to bother you, Kaiser. We've received a report you're hiding illegal contraband on the premises and have been sent to investigate." It was a bare-faced lie, but well within the confines of Drazah's jurisdiction. "Is your paramour home?"

"She's upstairs." Kaiser Ram turned over his shoulder and called up to her. "Kithoe, could you come downstairs, please."

"Thank you." Drazah smiled as if to apologise for the inconvenience.

Behind him, Drazah's men congregated around the carts. The horses bickered as they waited impatiently, drawing the kaiser's eye to the pyre they brought with them.

"Busy day?" he motioned to the cart with cold, dead eyes.

"And how. Wish I knew what I've done to earn my dad's scorn, he's got me running errands all over Halda today."

Kaiser Ram laughed with him, but it was as disingenuous as the pleasantries Drazah exchanged with his paramour when she joined them.

Kithoe Ram was not at all as Drazah expected her to be. Sudran women were often as powerful if not more so than the men, but Kithoe actually appeared so. Her limbs were thick with solid muscles and she made no attempts to withhold her mana as others would. The edge of her blazing aura pressed against his own, wild and untamed. It was a brazen insult to everything Drazah was sworn to protect and only worked to assure him they were in the right place.

"I'm sorry to put you both out, but you understand we must investigate everyone, no matter their position."

"Of course, Your Highness," was all they repeated, unable to say anything more. Had Drazah sent some lowly guard they would no doubt have been far less co-operative, but then he wouldn't get to enjoy the sweat upon Kaiser Ram's brow.

Drazah smiled. "How about we get out of their way and take a seat in the study?"

"Great idea," Kaiser Ram agreed, his voice raised to distract from his paramour's worry. "It's just through here."

Drazah led the way, his confidence growing. By all outward appearances, the kaiser's home was perfectly normal. Too normal. It was no surprise to him there was no need for staff, because there was nothing for the staff to tend. The furniture was all straight and clean. The windows were dressed with pretty fabrics, and dark tapestries hung from the walls, but there was no mess nor clutter.

Drazah claimed the chair behind the desk and motioned for the couple to sit across from him. There were two bookcases against the wall behind him and Drazah watched their eyes to see which they tried to avoid. Kithoe Ram watched Drazah with intense orange eyes and a mouth so tight it was basically a knot, but Kaiser Ram avoided eye contact at all costs.

"Don't worry, I've instructed them to be careful. We're only here to appease the report."

"Thank you, Highness."

Drazah picked at the skin around his nail as if bored. He gave no such orders but did tell his men to make quick work of it. If their intelligence was to be believed, then everything of importance was hidden just beyond one of these bookcases, anything else his men found was of no importance.

"Such a lovely home you have here, I've half a mind to leave the city myself. The palace is great but the plateau is such a pain to climb each day." Drazah leant over the table and lowered his voice, a devilish glint in the azure of his eyes. "And between you and me, it's seriously lacking in storage."

Kithoe finally broke their contact, her eyes darting to his right.

A purr rippled through Drazah's subconscious as he leant back. He cracked his knuckles and left the couple to stew, while the men tossed and turned the rest of the building. Metal clattered and wood groaned, sandals smacking against the sandstone and tile floors as his men stormed one room and then the next.

Sabutok entered the study a while later and shrugged his lips. "All good here, My Lord. Want me to have the lads ship out?"

Kaiser Ram released a breath, but Kithoe never dropped her defences. Her features remained hard as stone and refused to break. It called to the demon in Drazah, to the side of him which craved battle and blood. They were locked in a battle of wits and Kithoe thought she was winning. It was time to correct that.

"Sabutok, call the men in."

Drazah watched the couple with increasing amusement,

smiling as if they were having a party. He rather regretted leaving Nymati at home, but she could likely feel his anticipation through the parabond.

"You two," Drazah lifted his chin, "Move the bookcase."

Kaiser Ram went pale and tried to stand but Sabutok held him down by the shoulder. Kithoe braced as the two soldiers grabbed the bookcase from either side and slid it to the middle of the wall, revealing a door.

Drazah popped his brow, a smug smile sliding back to the kaiser. "Well, what do we have here?"

Drazah leapt from his seat like a cat offered cream and pushed on the door, only to find it locked. He looked over his shoulder to the kaiser, but said nothing. Instead, Drazah activated the mana residing in his body. He called it to his hand and slammed his fist against the lock, splintering the wood as it shot into the room beyond.

The door creaked on its hinges, opening to a room with no windows. Candles flickered upon an altar, the light licking the marble of a strange totem carving in the likeness of a beast with the body of a lion and the head of a bird. Jars of herbs filled the shelves and empty mortars were stacked upon a workbench. There were books and scrolls, an empty cauldron, rune-etched trinkets and glass orbs, yet it was the floor Drazah could not take his eyes from.

A large circle dominated the floor, one with a five-pointed star in the middle and stark runes inlaid between the circumference. It was black against the sandstone floor as if it were burnt into its surface. Drazah crouched to inspect it closer, static prickling his fingers as he held his hand over the circle.

Without realising why, Drazah activated his mana and drew it to his hand. Light filled the burnt circle in response to his touch, and sparked with untamed power. He snapped his hand back and returned to the study, the grim reality of his success growing all too apparent.

Neither Kaiser Ram nor his paramour showed any remorse, just acceptance.

"Sabutok, have the men clear this room and erect the pyre in the garden."

"You can't!" Ram belted, but Sabutok held him firm.

"Oh, but I can." Drazah relished the power he had at that moment as he slowly padded across the room. He released a low menacing chuckle. "Why else do you think I packed the kindling?"

Kithoe squeaked as Drazah placed his hand on her head. She shook from breaths too short and sharp, her strength suddenly dimmed.

"Now then, I think it's time we have a more honest conversation. Don't you?"

* * *

Drazah rubbed his bruising knuckles as he left. Despite his efforts, Kaiser Ram and Kithoe refused to give up the names of other witches, giving Drazah no choice but to follow through on his warning.

His eyes to the ground, Drazah gave the order.

"Tie them both."

Drazah tried not to listen to their screams of protest as men dragged Kaiser Ram and his paramour to the pyre. He didn't want this. He gave them every opportunity to save themselves. The thrill of the hunt was one thing, but there was no honour in burning your enemies at a stake.

They did this to themselves, he told himself. It was for the good of his people, for all of Alamantra. There could be no peace while witches roamed Sudra freely.

Sabutok held out a flaming torch. "You want to do the honours?"

Drazah grabbed the torch, his face grim, but the sentiment was appreciated.

"You condemn Sudra to death without our power," Kaiser Ram cried from atop a pile of kindling. "Mark my words, you need us to survive the desert."

"Sudra needs witches like I need a scorpion in my bedsheets, Nurzi. Asphet-Kau created dark artes in defiance of the Gods and now you use them in defiance of your king. You are no prophet or saviour."

Drazah clenched his fingers around the torch to hide the fact he was shaking. He'd killed a man before, but never had he sent one to the flames. It was different somehow. Less righteous. There would be no coming back from this for him. Yet, it was what he must do for the sake of his people.

"I ask our lord Asphet-Kau for forgiveness and cast these witches into the flames."

Drazah threw the torch upon the kindling, the fire catching

upon oil and running along the twigs and branches.

"May you find peace in the next life."

The flames crackled and oil spat, roaring as it spread. Drazah shielded his eyes from smoke and turned away. His men watched in silence as he walked to the cart and removed a scroll, nails and hammer. Curses and cries filled the air behind him, thick black smoke blocking out the sun as Drazah unfurled the scroll and held it against the wall. His face set with a grim determination, he hammered each corner.

"Men, pack up and take this lot back to the palace," Drazah ordered, waving at the carts without checking to make sure they heard him.

He dawdled along the road back to the palace, not really caring about his horse or company, and left the notice for all to see:

> *Heed our final warning.*
>
> *We know who you are.*
>
> *Put an end to all dark artes and sorcery*
>
> *and we shall let you live.*

* * *

Drazah left Sabutok to oversee the confiscated items being offloaded and lifted to the palace. He mounted the plateau stairs, skipping up two or three at a time in his eagerness to tell his queen of their success. But it seemed word had already reached the palace.

Drazah's father, King Ushmi Tamun stood upon the plateau, his mouth cut into a thin line above the square of his jaw. Often times Drazah thought looking at his father was like looking into his future, but on this occasion, he saw only scorn.

Nymati lingered in the king's shadow. Her eyes levelled with Drazah's, calm and serious. Drazah feared the weight of the planet about to drop upon him, yet she appeared untroubled. If anything, she seemed more assured of herself than before.

"My office. Now," his father boomed and walked away.

Drazah swallowed and began his pursuit, Nymati falling in beside him. She slipped her fingers between his, her palm ever warm against his as the gentle tingle of her charm eased his nerves. Then all it took was the slight press of her ebony lips and suddenly nothing seemed impossible any more.

The king held an office on the ground floor of the palace. It was a stuffy room filled with too many shelves and bookcases lined with stacks and scrolls of various records. Drazah thought it the worst room in the palace save the dungeons. It was always dark despite the tall windows overlooking the city and couldn't catch a breeze in a sandstorm.

King Ushmi sat behind his desk, quietly tapping his fingernail upon the surface as he thought.

Drazah chewed his lip. He would be at a disadvantage if he spoke first, so it was better to wait, yet the silence was excruciating. It regressed him back to his youth, to when he was being scolded for misbehaving, but Nymati squeezed his hand before letting it go. Drazah's strength was doubled. In the face of his father, Drazah was just a prince, but with Nymati by his side, Drazah was a king. A king who just rid their kingdom of a great foe.

"It is one thing to conduct an investigation behind my back, but to go after one of the most influential kaisers in Halda without first consulting me is a level of lunacy I never thought my own blood capable of." King Ushmi pressed his palms against the desktop, bracing as he drew a deep measured breath, then sighed. "I take it from the smoke you hailed successful."

"Yes, Father." Drazah bowed his head. "They had a hidden chamber filled with horrible monuments and tomes. There was even a circle on the ground which they used to perform their rites. I confiscated the lot and put the estate under the crown's control."

Nymati's head turned inquisitively towards him at this, but she held her thoughts.

"You foolish children," King Ushmi hissed. "What will you do if the witches decide to retaliate over this?"

Drazah lifted his chin in defiance. "You say that as if they aren't already rioting through our streets each night. The common folk are scared to leave their homes. Sudra are being murdered daily and rotten flesh drops from the heights of our palace. What more do you expect them to do, Father?"

"Why do you wish to test them?"

"I say, let them come, but I don't think they will." Nymati placed her hand upon Drazah's shoulder to call back his temper. "These covens preach organised religion disguised as family - until now we have been playing with their children. I should imagine they're running scared without their mother and father."

"That's if it was, as you say, their parents you burned today." Ushmi folded his thick arms across his chest. "What more has your inquiry freed from the sand?"

"Um." Drazah cleared his throat to save himself from tripping over his words. "We sent men across Sudra in hopes of infiltrating the various covens. This was the first to come back to us with a name. Additionally, we now know some covens chose to mark their members with runes to identify themselves."

"But not all of them?"

"We've not checked them all to be sure."

King Ushmi sucked his fangs. "Very well. I will allow you to continue your investigation. Time will tell if I was right to do so."

* * *

Drazah was determined to prove himself, but was left to the mercy of the secret army.

The women would report to Nymati, disguising themselves as her staff in order to slip by unnoticed. The men reported to Drazah, often on his way to the training grounds or when he and Sabutok stopped by the Sand Wrym for a drink. Their appearances were few and far between, however, and King Ushmi was an impatient man.

He called both Nymati and Drazah back to his office only

two weeks later, his expectations high. His nose pinched and his face soured as if chewing on a lemon, peering over pressed fingers from behind the desk.

"I won't deny things have calmed down this side of the river, but the witches still run amok in The Narrows. There's now word of some witchling calling it a haven and encouraging others to cross the river."

"I had the bridges manned day and night, Father, and caught several trying to pass on boats, but the witches are running scared and are proving more difficult to infiltrate as we did before." Drazah had done much besides but none of it would be enough to appease his father.

"So you have nothing to report? Gah!" Ushmi threw a hand up as if to dismiss them. "I should have known this was going to happen. You should've come to me, instead of running around playing at witch hunter."

Drazah's lip curled, his fingers tightening into fists. He was ready to give his father a piece of his mind, but Nymati got there first.

"Actually, Your Grace, we have the names of two coven leaders, but thought it best to wait on further proof before troubling you."

The calculation in Nymati's honeyed tones were sharp as spear points as she patted Drazah's arm. She was just as infuriated with being treated like a child as Drazah was, but was infinitely better at hiding it.

"If it would please Your Grace, I would be happy to share their names."

This was the first Drazah heard of any news from their secret army, but he wasn't going to share that. Even if it were a ruse, Drazah trusted in his queen's handling of all matters.

"Well, out with it then."

"Of course." Nymati dipped her head, obedient. "The first should be of no surprise to you, Sandlord Orim of the Burning Wastes."

"Orim? Ah, yes, we've had our eye on him for a while now but have had no reason to disturb him while he keeps to the sands. What about the other?"

Nymati ran her tongue between her fangs as she looked at him, sucking up the courage to say the name. "Lila Kol."

Drazah furrowed his brow, unable to place the name, but he recognised it.

"Kaiser Kol's paramour?" King Ushmi righted himself, his chin raising with his concerns. "That's some accusation."

"And I told you I sought further evidence to affirm my claim." Nymati matched his gaze, calm as a desert oasis, but she held his attention, and she knew it. "If our messengers are to be believed, he runs the mines and she runs the village as a safe haven for witches. We may even find a number of high-profile fugitives among their staff."

A cold shiver ran down Drazah's spine as the pair squared off against each other. Nymati may not have held the strength of the king, but her power was undeniable. His father was a giant compared to Nymati and the most powerful man in Sudra, yet she stared right back at him, unblinking.

"You trust your sources?"

"Implicitly."

A low growl rumbled at the back of King Ushmi's throat as he adjusted his weight.

"There's no proof Kaiser Kol has any involvement in this, of course. However, I would like to remind Your Grace of the hold the good lord of the land has had over his mines of late."

A smirk passed from Nymati to his father, her suggestion clear. The mines in Tagrin were rich in iron, but Kaiser Kol hoarded it for himself and traded only in forged weapons at higher prices. This forced the crown to buy minerals from elsewhere or take the hit to their coffers, neither of which gained him any favour.

King Ushmi released a full-bellied laugh. "Fine, have it your way. I'll have the army swing by for an inspection and see what they uncover."

"Thank you." Nymati bowed.

"Would you like me to lead a party, Father?"

"No, I want you two to remain here and focus on The Narrows." King Ushmi nearly smiled. "Let's show these witches there is nowhere they are safe."

* * *

Drazah's praises left him as they entered their room.

"You were amazing in there."

He wrapped his hands around Nymati's waist and pulled

her close.

"My love, my life, what did I ever do without you?"

Drazah showered her with kisses. They moved as one across the room, his tail coiling around her thigh in a flickering dance of heat and tenderness. Nymati opened her mouth with a silent moan, Drazah's tongue lapping her pointed ear as she writhed to his touch.

He whispered, "Together we will rid Sudra of witches and live in history beside Asphet-Kau and Anneke-Sun until the planet stops turning."

"We will rule Sudra like no one before." Nymati's nails raked through his hair, her artes activated to encourage him on as Drazah's hands rounded her breasts. "We'll take out every last coven if that's what it takes. You and I."

"You and I," he repeated. *He liked the sound of that...*

* * *

Full Bloom

Spring Year 3658 - 17 BMF

* * *

More often than not,

it was the times of peace I found the most interesting.

For I wondered if it could truly be called peace

when you know all that was going on beneath the surface.

* * *

Prince Callius Gabris was a young man in his prime. Dressed in the traditional Duran armour of a polished bronze chest plate, brown studded leather lappets and bronze galea, he swung a wooden shortsword at his cousin, Tidus, who matched him, under the watchful eye of Sir Maximus Melus, Captain of the Palace Guard.

"Again," Sir Melus called as the wood of their blades clashed. He was an aged Dura with a shock of silver hair and brilliant blue eyes. In his youth, he was considered quite handsome, yet the years were hard on his features, leaving them to droop.

Callius cast his shield aside and held his sword in both hands. The tanned muscles of his arms bulged and flexed to accommodate the weight, his hips and feet turning into a stronger stance. His eyes levelled with Tidus, the solid jade green of his iris reflecting the calm of his mind.

The yellow light of spring lined his blade as Tidus ran in with his next attack. Callius lifted his shortsword, wood smacking left and right in a futile barrage of swings. It was foolish of Tidus to throw his sword so wildly but it worked to Callius' advantage as he bat each attempt away effortlessly. A battle wasn't won with blades alone, it was won with patience and wit. A lesson Tidus was soon to learn.

Callius side-stepped as Tidus threw his weight behind his latest attack. Missing, Tidus followed through, but his draining energy left him clumsy and he tripped. Dust rose from the impact of Tidus landing on the ground. He huffed and rolled to his back, looking up to Callius along the wood of his shortsword.

"I yield." Tidus threw his hands up, grinning.

Callius smirked but it was short-lived as Sir Melus smacked him around the back of the helm.

"What have I told you about using your sword like that? The only reason your blade's not shattered is that they're made of wood. One chip and your steel will fracture and you'll be dead."

"And I keep telling you, I'll have a sword made big enough to withstand any blow. Just as soon as I can find a blacksmith willing to make one." Callius pulled off his helm and rubbed the back of his head. His father refused to let him wield anything larger than a short-sword and word had passed through the forge masters, deterring them from accepting his request.

"You're not yet ready for a greatsword, Young Prince. If you skip to something so heavy too fast, it will only give you problems when you're older. Assuming you don't get killed before then, that is." Sir Melus took the training sword from Callius. "Once you're fully grown I shall see to it you get a sword befitting you."

Tidus removed his helm and released a mane of straight blonde hair which fell into curtains about the sharp points of his cheeks. He scoffed and looked Callius up and down. "How much bigger d'you want him to be? He's already two hands taller than I am."

"Might be three now." Callius ran a hand from the top of his head to the air above Tidus.

"Mark my words, His Majesty was thin as twigs when he was your age. Just look at him now." Sir Melus wiggled his finger at them with his warning. "Now away with the pair of you. You're to get ready for tonight."

"Whey hey," Tidus cheered. He passed Melus his sword and threw his arm around Callius. "Let's hit the baths, cousin. We don't want to stink of sweat and scare away the women."

* * *

The bathhouse was a private facility at the back of the palace. Designed to be the most lavish bathhouse in all of Rhoda, it boasted warm lounging pools, saunas, cold pools and an array of masseurs and aids on hand to see you well.

Callius called upon the staff to remove their armour and dropped his underwear before walking into the showers. Scrubbing and scraping, he and Tidus removed all evidence of their training, and only entered the baths once they were clean. The pair swaggered, nude and confident in their youth and masculinity, and pretended not to notice the young ladies at the other end of the pool.

The water barely covered his stomach muscles as Callius sat down. He remembered a time when he and Tidus could swim in these waters, but it was a different kind of adventure they sought these days.

Tidus leaned into his ear. "I don't recognise them. Do you?"

"No, they must be here for the ball though. Probably some lord's daughters," said Callius. There were a number of lords and their families staying at the palace for the ball.

"Shh shhh. They're looking this way." Tidus grinned and flexed to a chorus of giggles. "We should go over and introduce ourselves."

Callius checked the ladies again through his periphery. One had hair of golden ringlets and the other two black. He was sure he didn't recognise them, but neither could he see well enough through the steam to be sure.

"Did you not learn from the last time you approached women in the palace, cousin?"

Tidus hissed with betrayal. "How was I supposed to know we were related? Not a single Gabris has hair that red. I'm still not convinced, and I'd bet three gold her mother was sneaking out on our Uncle Duronius."

"I'll take that bet, but only if I get to be there when you ask her." They shook on it and watched as a Sudran woman in a plain dress entered.

The Sudra had always been somewhat of a curiosity for the young prince. With dark skins like charcoal, forked tails and pointed horns above their temples, they were the opposite of the Dura in many ways, yet held a similar general build. This particular Sudra had long grey hair tied into a ponytail and eyes a mix of pink and red to match an evening sky. She was pretty enough, but having met their princess, Callius struggled to see any other Sudra as beautiful. There were few reasons Callius could think of for this Sudra to be in his bathhouse, yet she strode the tiled floor with a stack of towels and firm confidence which allowed her to cross to the pool unhindered.

"Your towels, My Lady." The Sudra bowed and set the towels on the bench. "Would you like me to come back?"

The golden-haired one conferred with her friends before answering. "I think we're done. Could you pass me a towel?"

"Yes, My Lady."

The Sudra held a towel open for the golden-haired one first. Callius watched without breathing. Water slipped away from her naked body like liquid diamonds, glittering droplets tracing the curve of her hips to the squeeze of her thighs.

Callius left his jaw skimming the water as the three ladies wrapped themselves and left for the changing rooms.

Tidus splashed water at him. "Careful, cousin. You stare any harder and she'll wind up pregnant."

Callius splashed him back. "You child."

Tidus swung his arm to grab Callius by the head and dunk him, but Callius caught him first. He flipped Tidus over his shoulders and let him crash into the bath water. Tidus returned laughing and pushed his soaked hair from his face.

"Please remember yourself, Your Highness," scolded the elderly attendant.

Callius ducked his head in false remorse, "Sorry."

Tidus sniggered. "Yeah, Callius."

* * *

Callius shook out the chest of his toga to ensure it lay just right over his pectorals. He worked hard to maintain his physique and thought himself mildly handsome, but held enough humility to be quietly nervous in the face of Duran socialites.

"Prince Callius Gabris, first of his name and heir to the throne." The herald announced Callius as he entered the throne hall.

Those close to him bowed and moved away, allowing him to cross to the dais where the thrones seated their king and queen. The dais worked as a barricade between his parents and those welcomed into their presence. Couples danced beneath the giant candelabra and others mingled all around the walls, yet his parents remained on their thrones. Silent. Watching. Judging. It was not something Callius was in a rush to partake in.

"Mother. Father." He bowed and smiled upon his return. "I hope you're having a pleasant evening."

"Your cousins have yet to start arguing, so there is that," his mother offered. Queen Camilla was often described as beautiful by their citizens, but Callius failed to see it. She studied him like a reptile. Eyes cold as ice looked him up and down, a dress of navy and sapphire-coloured satins flowing from around her long neck and flaring out by her feet. "What happened to the clothes we sent you?"

"I received no clothes," he lied, "And you told me I wasn't to wear my armour."

"The point of these functions is for us to get better acquainted with our people, not to flash your promotion. You will forge friendships into lifelong allies who would give their life for your orders, but they must first see you as a man before they will learn to respect you." King Linus Gabris spoke in long, well-thought-out sentences, but often lacked the softer edges of wisdom. "Or do you intend to continue running around with scoundrels in the dive bars with your cousin?"

Callius gleamed without shame. He and Tidus were notorious for sneaking from the palace to the taverns without guards. Thankfully, his father had been no better at his age.

"Just do me a favour and keep out of trouble while your uncles are still lurking." King Linus gestured to his brothers who sat on his Council. "Snakes, the pair of them."

Queen Camilla placed her hand over his, "Come now, Dear. This is not the place for such fancies."

King Linus grumbled and cast doubts under his breath. It was no secret to anyone the Gabris Uncles had an eye for the throne. They were, after all, next in line after Callius. Their family line ran all the way back to Zorum, first of the Dura, but it was a bloody history wrought with as much infighting and betrayal as not.

Callius bowed.

"I shall do my best to see nothing disturbs your peace."

Having escaped his parents, Callius decided to ease his mood with some fresh air.

The great hall opened out onto a veranda crawling with ivy where guests gathered. Steps led down into the gardens, the flowers green and budding in a maze of flowerbeds, but Callius followed a familiar voice to the veranda benches.

Tidus perched on the railings, his crimson toga opened to expose his chest and the top of his well-formed stomach. Dimpled cheeks and exaggerated hand gestures conducted the attention of three ladies seated on the benches, the ones from the bathhouse.

"Cousin, there you are. Come. Join us. Let me introduce you." His enthusiasm suggested Tidus had a head start on the wine.

He introduced the two ladies with black hair as sisters, the daughters of Lord Festa from Tennu, a rural area towards Estra. They shared a similar rectangular shape and straight black hair but Ponita, the eldest, had hazel eyes when Axia's were closer to green. Callius thought them pleasurable enough but fell impatient waiting for Tidus to introduce the woman with the golden curls.

"And this is Marella, the daughter of Lord Messor."

Callius pressed his brows. Messor was known as a notorious recluse with a foul personality before his passing. "I wasn't aware Lord Messor had any children."

"Not legitimately at least," Marella barbed, a deep fire in the amber of her eyes. "Gave my mother two children, but wouldn't make an honest woman out of her 'til he was old and unable to care for himself."

"Still, better late than never."

"Too right. It's most certainly our gain to have you here with us tonight." Tidus flashed his cheek dimples in a way certain to make the ladies titter.

Callius allowed Tidus to take charge of the conversation and leaned on the railing beside him. They worked well together when finding women in bars, but the rules changed among those in high society. He was their prince, who would one day soon become king, which made him God among the common folk. The men and women of the upper echelons of Duran society, however, commanded as much respect as himself, often more. They were renowned scholars and artisans of the highest calibre, high lords, knights and heirs to vast fortunes. He was their prince, but he was not their equal.

Marella giggled and raised a hand to cover her mouth. "My Prince, you have something on your arm."

Callius recoiled at the fuzzy green caterpillar crawling over his bicep toward his armpit.

"Ugh, I bloody hate these things." He flicked the insect away. "I swear, the first thing I'm doing upon becoming king is ridding the palace of them. We can tear the whole garden out if that's what it takes. I'll have them put in a pool and some loungers."

"Heck yeah. Wine fountain in the corner." Tidus pumped his fist. "Right next to the kitchen. I'm in."

"I would be sad to see the gardens go," said Marella. "The flowers are already so beautiful, I imagine it only doubles when in summer bloom with the butterflies dancing about them."

"Y- Yeah. I guess it is." His ears burned.

"Ignore her, cousin, a pool is an excellent idea." Tidus rallied the two others to his cause but Callius was no longer listening.

He smiled and Marella smiled back, their gaze united. Panic filled his chest, his thoughts blank as Marella wet her lips. She pouted, movement rolling her back from her shoulders through to her hips, like a leopard through the shadows.

Callius swallowed, his manhood throbbing like a stubbed toe. Was he a fool, or was she flirting with him? What should he do?

If this were some back-alley tavern and Marella some drunken wench, he would merely descend upon her with everything the Gods gifted him. But this was not a tavern and Marella was no wench. She was a lady. One deserving of care and proper decorum. Anything less would be an insult, and sure to cause him much trouble with his parents within eyeshot.

His options few, Callius chose the least objectionable and summoned his courage in the face of rejection. He held his arm out to Marella with his offer.

"My Lady, could I interest you in a dance?"

Callius lost the ability to breathe with his heart climbing so far up his throat. He waited, certain Marella planned to decline him as her hands clasped before her chest.

"It would be an honour." She bowed her head.

Static ran along his arm as Marella took Callius by the hand. He wrapped her arm around his and passed feigned promises to return, but they were forgotten as soon as they passed his lips.

* * *

Under the watchful eye of his parents, Callius guided Marella to the centre of the throne hall. He released her arm and bowed beneath the glowing candelabra.

"My Lady." He offered his hand.

"Your Highness." She curtseyed.

Callius slipped a gentle hand around Marella's waist, the fabric of her dress soft against his hardened palm. His cheeks flushed as she held his shoulder and their bodies grew close. Together they swayed to the gentle harp and lyre, a delicate drum beating the rhythm.

The music changed and the tune gained pace. Callius knew the steps and counted them in his head so as not to miss one. He devoted all his focus to dancing, afraid he might crush Marella's feet with one misstep.

They danced and danced until their faces grew red and their legs tired. They grew closer and closer as the evening passed and the festivities drew to a close.

"This is nice," Callius finally managed now the dancing required him only to sway back and forth.

Marella giggled. "I'm glad. You were so quiet I worried I

bored you."

"Just trying to keep up, I assure you. You're a wonderful dancer."

"My father insisted I learn when he decided to try and marry me off. I didn't appreciate his reasoning, but I'm glad I've had the chance to put my lessons to use."

"I'm glad too." Callius smiled. He was also glad whatever marriage her father was planning appeared to have failed. "I wonder how your father would react to seeing you now."

Marella smirked, a sinister glimmer in her eyes. "I'm sure he's spinning in his grave."

Shivers called Callius to the attention of her cruel calculation and he missed a step. Their thighs brushed as they stumbled together. Catching his breath in a panic to hide his eagerness, Callius stepped back and recovered their stance as the music changed pace. Marella's golden hair wove through the air as he spun her around him to avoid another couple veering their way.

She smiled and laughed, each gesture more exquisite and alluring than the last. Callius hoped for their night to never end, but as the dancers dwindled and the buffet tables cleared, a voice dashed through his dreams.

"Excuse me, My Lady." The Sudran aide from before shrunk in on herself as if to apologise for her appearance. "Lady Pontia retired. She is unwell and requests you tend her."

Marella didn't scowl or raise her frustrations, but her fingers clung to Callius as she swept from his embrace. "My apologies, My Prince. Lady Pontia was the one who brought me as her guest, I cannot deny her request."

Callius flustered, his words lost. His heart ran too fast and his mouth too dry. "Oh. Of course. Duty calls."

"Good night, Your Highness." Marella bowed and hurried away.

Callius remained on the dance floor, the hundred million things he wished to do and say leaving him still. Yet, he could not stop smiling.

* * *

"That's how you left it?" Tidus exclaimed the next morning in Callius' bedroom.

"Well, what was I supposed to do?"

"I dunno, something!"

Callius sighed. He didn't understand why he suddenly found everything so difficult. Was finding a woman to share his bed that much different than courting a lady? In his mind, all the steps seemed the same, yet somehow he always had much better success with the former than the latter. There was just too much to consider. The ladies he chased could one day become his queen, and it would do his reputation no good among his lords to make a quick conquest of their daughters.

"Should I invite her to dinner?"

"If only you had the time. They leave today."

Callius stood with sudden urgency. "Then I should go to her before they do."

"To her room? Bit forward don't you think?"

"Then tell me what I should do, Cousin." Callius waved his hands, exasperated. "What if we go wait for them by the carriages."

"No, that won't do at all." Tidus shook his head, but stopped, his fingers snapping upon an idea. "Let's invite them to join us for an early lunch. We can host them in the reception room as they await their carriage."

"I like it."

Callius scrambled through his drawers for a quill and paper to write his note. His heart beat to the sounds of ten thousand marching soldiers as he called one of the palace staff to take the note to Marella's room.

"What now?"

Tidus grinned and wrapped an arm around his shoulders. "Now, we change, Cousin."

* * *

Callius was a mix of emotions as he and Tidus arrived in the reception room. They were both dressed in their best cream tunics and crimson togas, the red and gold embroidery a flashy reminder of their status.

The mid-morning sun beamed through the tall windows, crimson satin curtains hanging from bronze poles and fastened with tasselled braids in the middle. Plush high-backed sofas and chairs surrounded a polished table where the palace staff placed a selection of finger foods and fruit. The portraits of many famous Gabris descendants watched over them, the one above the fire featuring Callius and his parents.

He claimed the corner of a sofa to allow him a clear view of the entrance hall and awaited their guests. Tidus sat across from him, naming it a ploy to split their guests between them to better engage.

"Relax, cousin. You look like you have a spear down your toga."

Callius scowled, but Tidus was saved from his response as the ladies descended to the entrance hall. They rose to greet them.

"Ladies, so good of you to accept our invite." Tidus held Marella's hand and guided her toward Callius before commandeering the two sister's attention for himself. "You all look radiant this morning."

That they did, and Callius was sure to agree. They each wore pale dresses which flowed to their feet but tied them in the middle with different coloured belts.

Marella blushed and curtseyed. "Good morning, Your Highness."

"Good morning. I take it you slept well?" He motioned for them to claim the sofa together. "I hope you've enjoyed your time with us."

Tidus sat between the two sisters across from them and started a conversation of their own.

"Very much so. The palace is most exquisite."

Callius thanked her and hoped her opinion of the palace extended to himself. "Did you get to visit much else of Rhoda?"

"Our carriage passed by the coliseum a few times and we visited the market, but our visit has been a mostly social one."

"That's a shame. Rhoda has a lot to offer, especially if you don't mind going off the main roads. There's art and music everywhere you look, if you know where to start." Callius picked a grape from the table and assembled his words. "I'd be happy to show you."

"That would be lovely. I've always wanted to visit the animal gardens, but have yet to find the opportunity."

"I can't believe you've never been to the animal gardens," said Callius. "A great many Duran scholars study the animals there. You're sure to find something to your liking."

"I hear they have a lion, I would love to see one someday. My mother always made them sound so spectacular."

Callius jumped at the opportunity to impress her. "If it's a lion you wish to see, then we have one here in the palace, but I'm afraid he's only a taxidermy."

Marella's eyes lit up. "You do?"

"I can show you if you like?"

"Oh, please." She clasped her hands before her chest. "If it's not too much trouble."

"None at all." He stood and held out his hand to help her from the sofa. "If you'll come with me, my Lady, I shall take you to him."

Callius smiled as her hand held his, but lost all feeling in his legs from the sudden rush of blood from his brain. He held his composure and wrapped her arm around his as they walked to the first of the palace trophy rooms. It was a dark and serious hall but held all the things his father considered important. Marble busts of long-dead kings lined the walls, backdropped by canvass depicting savage moments from history, each passing their combined judgements on any who passed.

"This way."

Marella gasped as he opened the door to the adjoining room. A taxidermy lion perched upon a giant rock in the centre of the hall. Its head was raised with pride, fur like golden sands and a mane so thick and well-tended it appeared to sway without a breeze.

Callius placed a gentle hand on the lion's back. "He's been in the family for generations. The great Denero Gabris was said to have wrestled it with his bare hands to preserve the coat and bring it home. It's supposed to bring the Gabris family luck to pet him before a battle."

"He's beautiful." Marella delicately stroked the line from the lion's nose to its ears. "And so soft."

Unsure what else he could say, Callius turned to the displays for the next item of intrigue. The armour and weapons of all the late great kings and their conquests were housed with the lion. He showed Marella them all, and she indulged his pride with each piece of history he shared with her.

"And what of this one," she asked, looking up at the biggest broadsword of the collection.

"This one is my favourite, it belonged to Herculous Gabris. I would have a sword to match this if only my father would let me." His fist curled with his bitterness.

"Aww, the one beside it is broken." Marella's body lilted as she noted the slender blade in the shadow of the broadsword.

"Ah, Kaeso Gabris. They say the tip of his blade remains in the chest of the Estra Chieftain he bested."

"Kaeso? Isn't he the one who died in the baths?"

Callius' confidence popped and his chest deflated as he snorted. "Tch. He annexed half of Estra before that, but yeah, that's what people remember him for."

Marella tipped her head to the side, the light twinkling in her eyes. "And what would you like to be remembered for?"

"I don't know. I guess I just figured things like that would come as they will."

"Do you only intend to landscape the palace gardens and forge giant swords in your regency?"

Callius cocked his brow. "Well, I've got to start somewhere."

She chuckled, but didn't seem entirely convinced by his answer.

Callius puffed his cheeks as he exhaled and searched a little deeper. "It would seem I have some thinking to do."

"Will you write to me if you find something?"

"I would need to find your address."

"Then I shall write you upon my return home and make sure you have it."

"I look forward to it. I-"

Again they were interrupted by the arrival of the Sudran handmaid. She bowed.

"My Lady, the carriage is here to take you home."

Marella lifted her skirts to curtsey. "This has been magical, Your Highness. Thank you so much for sharing with me."

Callius took her by the hand, placing a gentle kiss on the back. "I assure you, My Lady, the pleasure was all mine."

* * *

Both Callius and Tidus escorted the ladies to the carriage, like true gentlemen. They exchanged the last of their pleasantries and watched as the horses drew them away from the palace.

"Ssssssooooow," Tidus slid his eyes to Callius, his grin like a half-moon. "How'd it go?"

"You're hopeless." He pushed Tidus by the shoulder and turned back to the palace. "You know a gentleman never shares."

"Since when were you a gentleman?" Tidus jumped on his back, forcing Callius to catch him. "Don't tell me you went all shy on her."

Callius told him nothing. Not that day at least.

He wanted to keep that day special, for he planned to remember it. It was a day he would one day celebrate and hold dear for many years after:

The day he found his queen.

* * *

Arafrey's Mission

Spring Year 3667 - 8 BMF

* * *

Only in the face of adversity

does one discover who they are.

* * *

Princess Arafrey raised slender green fingers to cover her mouth. The emeralds of her eyes glistened as tears welled. She couldn't have heard that right.

Her mother stood before the glowing manapool of the city temple. The Life Tree grew behind her, its bark glowing with the soft mystic-blue hue of the Manastream converging in the atmosphere as it reached high above the forest canopy. High Priestess Elsafrey wore her crown of silver and diamonds, her hair flowing beyond her waist in waves of moss-green. She read from a scroll, her features pressed with concern.

"After negotiations broke down, His Majesty retreated from Alensya with a battalion but has yet to cross the Leste. Prince Timofrey and Commander Pendo lead our forces north to the border and we are to prepare for war."

Arafrey swallowed and nervous chatter passed between the temple sisters. She feared for her father. He was a warrior and a stubborn Frey, but even he would be meek as a babe if found lost and alone in a foreign land. Tensions between Freya and Sheya had been tenuous for years, but no one expected a simple trade negotiation to break down so terribly.

"Foot soldiers have been called to arms and volunteers are

to arrive at the Bourges Fort within the week to begin training. They've asked for any skilled in healing and medicine to hold triage in Mosswood."

Arafrey's heart skipped. Mosswood was the northern military base where Reyla was stationed, she was sure of it. While Arafrey was yet to forgive Reyla for leaving her employ to join the military, the thought of Reyla being thrust into war struck her sick. Forgetting her fury, father and kingdom, Arafrey's heart tugged with a far greater urgency.

She was already mentally packing her bags by the time Elsafrey dismissed them.

"Try not to worry, Dear. We'll see this is sorted out before anything terrible happens."

"Something terrible already happened. Father is lost in Sheya."

"I suppose, but he has good men with him. Commander Flaxel is with him, and Reyla too."

Arafrey's stomach nearly leapt from her mouth, the confirmation all she needed to fear the worst. "She is?"

"Hmmm," Elsafrey's smile seemed not to notice Arafrey's strife. She meandered through the courtyard between the pews to the temple. "And they're accompanied by a host of highly trained soldiers, who are there for just these incidents. We should be glad to have such wonderful Frey protecting us."

Arafrey agreed, but sitting around waiting for others to protect her was never something she was interested in doing. Being able to help and heal her people in the temple was the only part of her role she enjoyed, and now someone she cared for was in danger. She wasn't going to just sit about and do nothing. At the very least she could heal those injured on the battlefield.

"Don't even think about it." Elsafrey's eyes levelled with hers as if reading her mind. "You're not even twenty years old and could already be queen for all we know. As your mother and high priestess, I forbid you from going."

"What? That's not-" Arafrey's cheeks burned from the fire in her eyes. "You can't forbid me from going."

"I can and I have. I will hear no more on the matter." Elsafrey raised her hand, her palm flat as if to halt any further words. "Now I have much to do. I'll see you back at the palace."

Arafrey huffed and stormed from the temple, her mental inventory thrown into disorder in the process.

* * *

The skies were grey as wolf-pelts as Arafrey arrived back home, a palace grown from ancient trees. The drive was already lousy with carts and stacks of supplies as guards and handmaids emptied amours from the basement. Others from the Palace Guard already worked to repair and enforce the redwood arch of the entrance gates and used their artes to pull points from the tips of wooden poles they planned to set in the hedge as deterrents.

They may not have been on the front-lines, but war was upon them, her father was lost in Sheya, and in her heart, Arafrey knew Reyla was in the thick of it.

Arafrey's stomach lacked the strength for food, so she retired to her bedroom with the hopes of setting aside her worries with an early night. Her aide Keya was laying out a fresh night dress as Arafrey entered. She bowed, a straight platinum blonde bob sweeping her chin.

"Would you like me to bring you a bath, My Lady?" Each word was so softly spoken that Arafrey always had to concentrate when Keya spoke. Between Keya's white hair and milky eyes, it often felt as if Arafrey was tended by a ghost, although the ghost truly haunting her was one with hazel eyes and hair like a chestnut wildfire.

"Please."

Arafrey pinched the bridge of her nose, the call of a headache ringing in the distance. It had been a long day and a bath would be most welcome. She dropped to her bed and rubbed her knees through the linen of her robe skirt.

The firewood crackled and popped in the hearth as Keya set it alight and left to fetch the bath. It would take three aides to move, and as many to fill, but it was a small inconvenience when measured against the stress and labours of being the princess who would one day be queen and high priestess.

Besides, there would be no such luxuries in Mosswood.

* * *

By the time she rose the next morning, there was no question in Arafrey's mind of what she must do. She left her bed in the wake of dawn, the purple and blue lights of the sky turned umber through her curtains, and flung open the doors to her wardrobe.

The bedroom door creaked open behind Arafrey but she continued digging through the wardrobe.

"Is everything all right, Princess?" Arafrey could hardly hear Keya with her head beneath satins and skirts.

"Keya, bring my boots and cloak. Something light for horseback. Have you seen my satchel? The blue one."

"Princess?"

"Please. I don't have time for your questions. Do you know where I put my satchel or not?" Arafrey pressed her hands to her hips as she left the wardrobe to face Keya.

"No. I'm sorry, Princess."

Tarrek Valren was her guard that morning. He peered around the bedroom door, the chocolate curtains of his hair waving as he leaned to see what all the commotion was about. "Everything all right?"

"Shut the door behind you," Arafrey hissed, "Have you seen my satchel?"

"Planning on going somewhere are we, Princess?" Tarrek's father was close with hers and their familiarity allowed him some degree of informality. Still, Arafrey wasn't in the mood for him this morning.

"I'm going to Mosswood."

Keya gasped. "You can't."

"Don't worry, I don't expect you to come with me, Keya. I

know you have your brother to care for." Arafrey returned to the wardrobe to continue her search.

"But, Princess, who will dress you and tend your care?"

"Ah-ha!" Arafrey pulled the navy satchel from the depths of her wardrobe and began loading it with fresh clothes. "I'm going to Mosswood to be a healer, not a princess. If I take travel clothes and robes which tie in the front I should be able to care for myself well enough."

"I take it you've not run this plan of yours past your mother." Tarrek looked her up and down with a look more like his father than he'd appreciate knowing. He knew her well and knew full well her reasoning had nothing to do with healing.

Arafrey eyed him, her guilt clear, but it was the story she intended to keep. She wasn't even sure why it was so important to her she made sure Reyla was all right. What would she do if she arrived to find Reyla alive and well? What would she do if she found out the opposite?

A pain throbbed above Arafrey's temple, the thought of waiting to find out far worse than the fear of any harm that may come to her. "Do you intend to stop me?"

"I am your guard, Princess. Where you go, I go." He placed an arm across his chest and bowed his head. "I suppose you'll be wanting me to ready our horses?

"Thank you. I will make sure you take no blame for this."

"Then I shall bring them along the road and we can join the convoy. No one should question it if we act like we're supposed to be there."

"Keya?"

The aide pressed her lips and sighed. "Her Grace already left for the temple. If you leave now, no one will stop you."

Arafrey wrapped her arms around Keya and hugged her close. "Thank you."

"Don't thank me too much, I will deny seeing you if Her Grace asks."

"Then I never saw you either."

* * *

In the fresh air of morning, Arafrey threw her leg over the back of a tan mare with a cream mane and tail. Now dressed in a leaf-leather waistcoat, a thick woollen cloak and leggings, she looked no different than the many Frey gathering by the gates awaiting departure.

Tarrek drew in beside her upon a black stallion, his shield hooked to his leg and his sword resting down the horse's belly. "Commander Dondald leads the convoy. He'll be in the front. It would do us good to hang back and avoid him, at least til it's too late to turn back around."

A horn sounded outside the palace gates and the commotion of the Frey waiting subsided. Shuffling feet and raised supplies chorused along the road towards the Cross-Road Pavilion as a rippling wave of activity shifted them forward.

"Ready, Princess?"

"Let's go."

Arafrey nudged her horse into a trot and wove between the foot soldiers and medics into the heart of the convoy. Those around her took notice, it was not common for Frey to use horses but they would make an exception for her. Even though she wore travel clothes and had her hair tied above her pointed ears in tight braids, she was still Princess Arafrey, her porcelain skin and emerald eyes reflecting the authority of the high priestess she someday planned to be.

Travelling was by no means easy, and sleeping on the ground in bedrolls left much to be desired, but it was a small price to pay to set Arafrey's worries to rest.

Word reached them in whispers as King Galafrey's escape from Sheya passed through the convoy. The reports were mixed and confused, but Frey mobilised along the river Leste and sentried the bridges, stopping any Shey from crossing. His battalion was ambushed in Alensya, but no mention was ever made of anyone else returning with him. Arafrey heard many stories of how the war had started, none of them entirely true but all of them equally as haunting. All of them ended in a last stand on the border where everyone but the king fell, only to be saved at the last minute. It turned her stomach.

A pit grew there, one so deep Arafrey could think of nothing else. Her father was safe and leading their men on the front lines, but where was Reyla? Why did no one know where she was? Sure she was mad Reyla joined the army without telling her, and her resulting silent treatment had proven that, but that didn't matter anymore. She just wanted to make sure Reyla was safe.

By the time they arrived in Mosswood, it had been twelve days since the war began. The once quiet Northern village was now overrun with soldiers and passing enforcements. Local Frey assisted in their efforts, erecting fortifications on the outskirts and crafting leaf-leathers and steel to pass out. Even children and grandparents were drafted in to help with sewing and sealing, weaving and working. No one was left waiting.

Arafrey rode her horse to the temple doors, a free-standing grow with a silver bell hanging from a large oak tower. When compared to the temple in Ceynas it looked more like a chicken coop, with two single-storey healing wings branching from either side of the prayer hall.

The temple wards overflowed into the main hall, where beds were lined in close proximity to get as many in as possible. Arafrey scanned them from the entrance. It was hard to tell who they were, but general body size alone cut the number of potential Reylas down to only a few, and she ventured further inside to take a closer look.

The first bed she came to was a young Frey man, he was younger than her by a year or two and was missing his left leg from the knee down. His body twitched in pain even though he slept. Arafrey held her hand over the bandaged stump and activated her artes. Her hand glowed a soft white as she placed her hand over the wound and soothed his pains with her healing artes. Arafrey's lip curled, the ripped flesh and shattered bones responding to her touch were ripe and trying to fester. The young man would survive if they tended him well, but he had a long road ahead of him.

Arafrey left the young man sleeping and sought out the next Frey. The second's outlook was less positive. The medics had done what they could but a large bandage wrapped his chest where he seemed to have taken a projectile, possibly piercing his heart or lungs. His eyes were open but he stared blankly at the ceiling, his lungs gurgling as he strained for each breath. Arafrey smiled at him but there was little she could do at this point, the rest was up to him.

She was about to check the next bed when one of the medics came running up to her.

"Oh, Princess, we heard you were coming."

Arafrey tensed, certain her mother would be furious with her.

"We're so pleased you've come all this way to help us. I'm sure you know what you're doing, but if not I'm Mave." The woman bowed, her apron stained with more smudges and splatters than any apron should have. "I'm just a sister in the temple, our priestess is in the cellars, but if there's anything you want just let me know."

Although the sister was wildly unkempt in a manner unbefitting a temple, the dark bags beneath Mave's eyes rescinded Arafrey's harsher judgements. "Put me to work, Mave. I'm here and ready to help."

"If you're sure, Princess. You're welcome to rest-"

"No, I'm ready now."

Mave was smart enough not to question the princess and smiled. "Then it's time we get dinner to these patients of ours, would you mind helping me pass out the plates, Princess?"

Arafrey was more than happy to help. She passed out as many plates as possible so she could get a peek at the patients as she flew by. Energy bubbled from her toes to her fingertips, each passing plate bringing her one step closer to finding Reyla.

She was excited and anxious as she came down to the last few beds, plates in hand, ready to find her friend, but Reyla wasn't there.

Arafrey dropped the plates on the patients' laps without even a smile and made her way back up the hall to see where she was needed next. There was something else mixed within the disappointment which followed Arafrey through the temple, something too horrible and selfish to give a name to.

Wasn't it a good thing Reyla wasn't injured in the temple? Her absence didn't mean anything for certain, except that Reyla simply wasn't there. It didn't mean anything. It didn't.

"Best leave them to their dinner. Follow me," Mave smiled leading Arafrey out of the main hall. "They normally use this as the priestess' office, but given the circumstances, we thought privacy was best."

The office was small but bright thanks to the large windows and thin drapes. Bookcases lined one wall and all the furniture was stacked up in front of them to make room for a single bed. Laying, completely still, bandaged and bruised, was a soldier with flaring chestnut hair. Arafrey's heart lurched and she ran to inspect the patient.

"Reyla! What happened?" She didn't know where to look. There were too many injuries to count.

"Last one standing they say. Saved the king and got a sword planted through her shoulder for her troubles. Would be gone too if the cavalry hadn't arrived in time." Mave wouldn't have been able to understand the pride and anguish this caused Arafrey, but neither did it matter.

"Has she been out all this time? Have you tried-?"

"We've tried everything, Dear. You're free to try yourself but at this point, it's a waiting game. She seems strong, she'll pull through, t'will just take time."

Arafrey's fingers coiled into a tight fist, the edge of her nails digging into her palms as she tried to restrain herself.

Time was not a luxury afforded to those at war.

* * *

The war raged on around them but the fighting seemed a world away despite the steady stream of injured Frey passing through the wards. Every day Arafrey tended those in the temple before treating Reyla's wounds. She cleaned and dressed Reyla's shoulder and worked tirelessly, using artes to speed the healing progress, but Reyla had yet to wake from her slumber.

Exhausted, Arafrey retreated to Reyla's room with her daily notices and set a stool by her bedside. Her uncle was taking his command west along the river Leste as the Sheya forces spilled along borders. She had a letter from her mother, one rife with disappointment and worry, and another from her father, his disapproving monotone echoing through the words on the paper. They were not happy with her decision to leave but were in no position to oppose her and begged she remained as far away from the fighting as possible.

That was fine with Arafrey. She had already accomplished everything she needed from her rebellion. Reyla was safe. Nothing else mattered to her.

Arafrey activated her artes around the notices. The paper

glowed as she encompassed them within her control. She pulled on the leaf and mud pressed and formed with artes to make the paper, and broke it down into its lesser ingredients. Moulding it all together, Arafrey squished the pulp together and reformed it, a tiny paper bird residing in her hand as she pulled it away.

Fully formed, Arafrey placed the dove on the bedside table alongside the others she made on her previous visits. There were sixteen. One for each day Reyla continued to sleep.

Arafrey guarded Reyla's perpetual slumber, desperate to return the many kindnesses Reyla had shown her over years of friendship and servitude. That's all it was, wasn't it? Despite their status, they were friends, weren't they? Arafrey thought perhaps Reyla could be her only true friend, the only friend she chose for herself and the only one who ever truly listened.

A gust of air burst from Reyla as her body jolted awake. Her eyes flung wide, hazel and scared.

"It's okay, you're safe." Arafrey ran to her aid, shushing and petting as her mother would if she woke from a nightmare. "Easy now. We're at war with Sheya and you took a beating, but you're safe. How- How're you feeling?"

Arafrey's brow pressed with concern as Reyla struggled against lethargy to find her words.

"Stiff and groggy."

Reyla winced as she tried to sit up and the dressings over her body strained. She wouldn't admit to the hurt though and breathed through it with gritted teeth.

"I-" Panic drained the colour from her green skin. "Why

can't I? I can't move my hand. My whole arm, it's numb."

Arafrey wet her lips and inspected the arm, running healing artes along the shoulder and down Reyla's back. She knew Reyla's injury held such risks, her collarbone had been cleaved in two and the wound gouged her back down to her waist. Had it been a straight hit Arafrey held no doubts Reyla would have died upon impact, but as it was, the injury likely cut the connection between her head and her arm and there was no telling if it would ever fully recover.

Arafrey didn't need to say anything, Reyla already knew, she could see it in her eyes. Their hazel fire grew dim and grey. She looked so defeated and lost, not at all the Reyla Arafrey knew and cared for.

"What good will I be as a guard if I cannot hold my sword?" Reyla shook her head and turned away.

Arafrey took Reyla's hand in hers. "We'll figure this out. You've done so much for me. Let me do this for you."

Reyla agreed, but was just being polite. There was no fight in her, just an empty space in her heart where her ambitions once lay.

"No really, you'll see." Arafrey petted Reyla's hands. "Whatever it takes…"

* * *

By her word, Arafrey remained by Reyla's side and managed her treatment.

She was a poor patient in most regards and refused painkillers, swearing there were others who needed them more. Yet darkness resided upon Reyla's heart, one Arafrey feared no amount of medication could heal.

After three months Reyla could hold things again and her energy levels were almost normal, but she could only use her arm for so long before the tremors became unbearable. Reyla's plight often brought her to tears as she feared for her future, but all Arafrey could do was sit and wait for the tears to pass. These times were the hardest for them both.

Although she never used it, Reyla would always have her sword on her or within arm's reach. It was nothing special, just the standard shortsword the military provided her with. So why did she cling to it? Arafrey didn't understand. There were plenty of guards around.

"What use will I be with just one hand?" Reyla asked no one as she stared down upon her feeble hands. "I joined the army to serve and now I can hardly serve tea. What good am I?"

It broke Arafrey's heart, but she was not about to give up on Reyla now. Not after she travelled so far to be reunited with her once more. It was time for her to try something new.

"You were never good to begin with, you were the best. At everything we ever did. And you will be again. Now, come on. Get up."

Arafrey waved her arms and ushered Reyla to her feet. She dipped into the corridor and returned with a pair of wooden training swords she had Tarrek bring from the barracks.

"Where'd you get them?"

"Doesn't matter." Arafrey threw one to Reyla.

Reyla started as she caught the wooden sword by the handle with her left hand, but Arafrey wasn't shocked in the slightest. She readied herself.

"You will fight me."

"Princess, I don't-"

"That's an order. Wartime or not, I am still your princess and you will do as I say." Arafrey lifted her chin, summoning every ounce of her authority behind her wobbling sword. "Now ready your sword."

Reyla rolled her eyes but was forced to deflect as Arafrey lunged forward. Their blades clattered as Reyla knocked it away. "Hey!"

"I said, fight me."

Reyla's stance shifted to her left, the ache of her shoulder restraining her to a smaller perimeter. Even a layman like Arafrey could see the years of dedicated training snapping into focus behind the point of her blade. One-handed or not, Reyla wasn't just a guard or a soldier, she was a warrior, one tested in the heat of battle who saved their king.

Arafrey only hoped Reyla would one day come to see that too.

* * *

Things became easier after that. It was almost as if they were back home in the Ceynas palace as Arafrey tended her duties and sparred with Reyla each night.

The war with Sheya lasted six months and five days in total. After countless losses and destruction beyond measure, the war was brought to an end when Queen Nedeena of Sheya became grievously ill. High Priestess Elsafrey begged the kings to set aside their squabbles and offered her aid if they agreed to a truce. That was the last Arafrey heard from her parents before the orders came to disband their camps and return home.

By the time the war ended, Reyla had some use of her arm but won something far more precious instead.

"Make sure your medic runs artes over your back as well," Arafrey fussed upon Reyla's departure. "Most of your skin is scarring over but if it begins to weep-"

"They'll need cleaning. Yes, I know, Princess. Thank you, but you need not worry about me so much. You've done an excellent job in tending my recovery." Reyla flashed a reassuring smile and suddenly everything felt all right in Alamantra.

Arafrey's heart rattled with a strange tingly sensation. She didn't want Reyla to leave again. She didn't want to be alone again. Pins and needles ran the length of her body, but she didn't understand why, or what it was exactly she was so desperate to say.

"But you'll let me know if you need anything, won't you?"

"I promise. Please, stay safe, Princess."

It wasn't until after their goodbyes, when Reyla turned to rejoin her battalion, that Arafrey knew.

She knew there was no one she trusted more than Reyla. That there was no one she cared for as much as Reyla. There was no one, no one, in the whole of Alamantra she felt more safe and secure around than Reyla. And Arafrey knew from then on, she would want no one else by her side.

She discovered a great many things in that moment, but deep down Arafrey was confused.

She continued watching as Reyla walked away, her chest swirling and swelling, her eyes stinging and ready to burst. Then, through the mass of hurried soldiers, Reyla turned. Her eyes locked with Arafrey's and she gave her reassuring Reyla smile. Then, she was gone.

Arafrey clutched her hands to her chest, hoping to contain the emotions residing there.

She had never felt that way before. Relaxed, happy and sad, but nervous, excited and exhilarated all at the same time. It was strange, but she liked it. She wanted to feel that way all the time, if only she knew what it was.

But of course, Princess Arafrey was destined to be the last to realise her heart's desire. She was, however, determined to find out.

* * *

Freying Hearts

Spring 3668 years - 7 BMF

* * *

They say there's power in words,

but some could move mountains

with the weight of their words left unsaid.

* * *

It was warm when Reyla left the Barracks that evening.

She combed green fingers through her chestnut hair in an unsuccessful attempt to tame the waving mane. The green cape of her uniform breezed behind her as she turned and marched to the Frey palace to begin her shift.

Reyla received her promotion after the war and had not long been on the Princess' Guard, but it felt good to be back in Ceynas. It felt right working for Princess Arafrey again and brought her one step closer to realising her dream: to become a Knight.

The light of The Life Tree guided her way as she crossed between the paddocks to the gardens. Yellow petalled lilies occupied the flower beds and small birds sang in the trees, yet Reyla ignored them all, her hazel eyes fixed upon the timber palace.

Grown from oak and fern, the palace was a living monument to Frey architecture. Built over three floors, towers branched off from the main structure and parapets were woven into their roofs which ran thick with leaves like the canopy. A greenhouse hung from the rear by a service door, living vines stretching out into translucent panels to allow the light to pass through. Having lived and worked around the palace her whole life, it was a second home to Reyla, yet something seemed amiss upon her approach that evening.

Reyla's eyes narrowed as they turned to the bedroom window at the very end of the second floor to find it dark. She thought it strange. Even if the princess had eaten in the dining hall with her parents, it was unlikely she would have stayed long enough to see the guard change. But, it seemed her room lay empty.

Assuring herself she was paranoid, Reyla entered the timber palace through the service entrance. There were still Frey in the kitchen as she passed by, each dressed in plain clothes and an apron, hastily cleaning so they could clock off for the evening. The door to the staff bedroom lay open beside it, where four bunks had been crammed into the windowless room. Some of the waiting staff were already in there, including Lorelle, Princess Arafrey's aide.

"The princess has tickets to see that new play by Mr Asrich, so we'll be doing that tomorrow," Lorelle bragged, to Reyla's frustration. Of all her replacements, Lorelle was the worst.

She grit her teeth and ascended the narrow staff staircase to the second floor, aiming herself towards the princess' room to begin her shift. However, as she turned the corner and the door came into sight, she realised there was no guard stationed for her to relieve.

Reyla breathed through her nose as she knocked on the door, her mind wandering as she waited. It was unusual but the relaxed staff she passed earlier kept her nerves in check; she was sure there would be some commotion had anything gone wrong.

Reyla knocked again.

Still nothing.

She poked her head around the door to find it empty and returned to the kitchen, where two Frey were still cleaning.

"Have you seen the princess?" she asked them, but they shook their heads in response.

Reyla turned on her heel and crossed to the staff quarters. She knocked before opening the door. Here she found three Frey women still gossiping with Lorell.

"Do you know where the princess is?"

"Haven't seen her all day," Lorell replied.

Reyla bit her tongue, bile bubbling in her belly as she pressed a smile. It was Lorell's job to know exactly where the princess was. As Arafrey's aide, Reyla knew the princess' schedule by heart and would never lose track of her and it took every ounce of restraint not to tell her as much.

"Did she not return from the temple for dinner?"

"I honestly couldn't tell you." Lorell shirked her features and returned to gossiping before Reyla could ask any follow-up questions.

She slammed the door behind her and turned to the foyer, her apprehensions creeping like a feline approaching its prey. A rippling doubt ran down her spine, her heart rate increasing with the pace of her feet as Reyla swept over the polished floor to the two guards stationed by the front door.

Reyla recognised them but didn't know them by name. They were merely palace guards and given no coloured cape as Reyla had been, but each wore the same leaf-leather armour and wooden arte-formed chest plate as her.

"Have either of you seen the princess?" she asked, catching the urgency in her tone. But neither of them had.

Now thoroughly concerned, Reyla lapped the ground floor. She rushed through the drawing room into the dining room, finding each of them empty. The throne hall was equally deserted to the point her harried steps smacked off the solid floors, but there were two guards posted outside King Galafrey's office.

These guards were clad in steel armour and white capes meaning they were knights of the King's Guard. Reyla paused, coveting the crisp white linen and considered asking them, but thought it best to make sure the princess was missing before worrying the King's Guard. Besides, their presence also indicated the king was in his office and Reyla wasn't about to disturb him unless she had proper cause to.

Reyla continued her lap, checking the greenhouse and returning to the foyer, fruitless and unsettled. Her chest tight, she prepared to raise the alarms but startled. She whipped around, realising there was one place she had left to check before daring to disturb the king.

She returned to the second floor, taking two steps at a time. She turned away from Arafrey's bedroom, gaining speed as she trundled down the darkened hallway towards the Library.

There was no guard stationed outside as Reyla rapped on the door and pushed it open. Her breath caught as the hinges creaked open.

The library was a dark room that was lined and divided by tall bookcases. Candles were held in glass cases along their edges but much of the light came from a roaring fire. And before the fire, in a tall backed chair, sat Princess Arafrey.

"There you are," Reyla breathed, her shoulders dropping as she beheld the princess.

Arafrey jolted, seemingly confused as she looked up from a thick book. She flicked her head around to the window to see the darkness outside.

"Oh. Is that the time? I didn't realise." Princess Arafrey apologised and returned to her book.

"I'll take it from here," Reyla told Nasir, whom she was set to relieve. "Valren wants to see you when you get back."

"Cheers," he replied, nodding his head as he passed.

Reyla watched as Nasir left the library for the corridor, leaving her alone with the princess.

"You had me worried there," Reyla confessed, a softness in her voice that she only found for the princess. "They'd have my job if I lost you."

"My mother set me a reading assignment," Arafrey explained, holding up the book in her hands as evidence. "Try as I might, it's just not going in. I've read this same page six times now."

"Did no one think to bring you supper?" Reyla scowled and took Nasir's post by the fire. "Nasir should've said something."

"You worry too much," Arafrey teased, her juniper-green lips peaking into a smile.

Reyla didn't argue and settled in her post as Arafrey returned to her book. As a guard there was little Reyla could do but retain her post and watch, but still, she found herself frustrated. She pursed her lips, silently cursing Lorell and her ineptitude. She would never have allowed her princess to miss a meal.

* * *

The fire grew dim as Arafrey continued her reading. It crackled on occasion, the only sound other than the irregular turning of pages.

Arafrey discarded the tome in frustration.

"Whoever this Talonis Wisher is, he's a terrible bore."

Reyla snorted. "Maybe you should take a break and have something to eat," she suggested. It was apparent to her that food and rest were exactly what the princess required, but Arafrey never took well to being told what to do.

"No, it's late. Everyone will be asleep by now," Arafrey sighed, pressing her fingers into her temples.

The princess was prone to headaches, a fact very few Frey knew. They only really happened when she was stressed or had a social event she wished to avoid, but they hit hard and left Arafrey in pain for days.

"Come on," said Reyla, collecting the book from the floor.

"Come on, where?"

"Just come. You'll see," Reyla smirked.

Arafrey raised to her feet, her arms hanging loosely to the side of her robes as she walked. She followed behind Reyla as she returned to the corridor, placing the book carefully on a bookshelf as they passed.

Reyla guided the princess through the quiet palace to the kitchen. The lights were now dimmed and the staff in bed. An oven was installed on the outer wall, with pots and pans hanging above it from a burdened shelf. Thick oak counters ran the rest with a rectangular island in the middle, their surfaces wiped clean.

"Now you sit here," Reyla instructed, pointing to a wooden stool with a sideways grin.

"What're you doing?" Arafrey asked taking the perch.

"You'll see," Reyla replied mysteriously, reaching into the cupboards for supplies.

Things hadn't moved in the years since she left for the army and she found everything without thinking. Reyla removed a knife from the block and carved slices from a loaf of bread. She tossed the waiting princess a glance as she reached for a jar of strawberry jam, her chest warming to see Arafrey watching with tired eyes. Strawberry jam was Arafrey's favourite, which Reyla knew.

"That's where I used to sit while my father baked." Reyla smiled despite herself. Both he and her mother worked in the palace for a long time.

"How is he?"

"Good," Reyla replied automatically, but caught herself in the lie. "Well, he isn't worse. The tonics have been helping."

High Priestess Elsafrey had been treating him as best she could, but Reyla's father grew frail with his age. It was nothing they could fix with artes or soothe with balms. Instead, they fed the disease with potions and tonics designed to ease his pain. However, Reyla was unsure how much they truly helped.

"I'm glad."

Reyla combined the bread slices into sandwiches and cut them diagonally down the middle. She then ducked into the cupboard for a plate to place them upon.

"Now follow me," Reyla instructed, collecting the plate and her shield as she aimed for the door.

This time Reyla guided Arafrey out of the palace and into the garden. They followed the stepped path through the lilies into the heart of the garden. Here there was a lilypad-filled pond where fireflies gathered and a bench woven from teak hunkered by the flowerbeds.

"Here," said Reyla as she motioned to the bench with the sandwich plate.

Arafrey pulled her skirt under her legs as she sat down and accepted the plate.

"Would you sit with me?" asked Arafrey quietly.

Reyla nodded her head. She readjusted her sword as she took a seat beside the princess, hanging her shield over the side.

Reyla watched the fireflies dance over the water as Arafrey ate. Their pearly lights reflected on the surface combining with the blue hue of The Life Tree above creating a pattern that looked like waltzing stars. It was magical.

"Somehow your sandwiches always taste better," Arafrey commented, reaching for another sandwich half. "Lorell makes poor tea too."

Reyla didn't respond. She always found it better not to comment on others unless painting them in a positive light... No matter how much she disliked them.

"Do you miss it?" asked Arafrey, her emerald eyes sparkling with the light of the fireflies.

"Being your aide? Sometimes," she admitted, looking up to the night sky to disguise the blush across her cheeks. "The hours were certainly better, although I don't miss laundry or filling your bathtub."

Arafrey snorted, putting her hand to her mouth to secure the contents. Reyla cracked a wide smile. It wasn't often the princess laughed so Reyla always felt accomplished when she triggered it.

"We do get to spend more time together, so I suppose it's better this way," Reyla added.

"But I'm usually asleep through your shift."

"Even so," she returned warmly.

It was true, but times like this Reyla wished she were a nobleman, or any man at all for that matter. She long harboured a kindling flame for her princess but knew the planet would stop turning before she could ever pursue it. Until that day, Reyla was happy to stay by Arafrey's side, in whatever capacity that may be.

Arafrey sighed in response, the colour returning to her cheeks as she finished a second half of sandwich. She offered the plate to Reyla, waiting for her to take one before reaching for a third herself.

They sat in silence, enjoying the moment as they ate.

Normally, Reyla found silence excruciating, but with Arafrey it wasn't so bad. She was usually so focused on trying not to say the wrong thing and appear strong it was near impossible to consider anything else. But, at that moment, she found only peace.

She finished her sandwich and brushed her hands against her leggings.

"So what was that book about anyway?"

"Ugh, plant anatomy," Arafrey moaned, throwing her head back in disgust. "It's worse than history."

Reyla snorted this time. She often joined in on Arafrey's history lessons during her time as an aide and it had been a formidable foe for both of them.

Arafrey released a groan and slumped over to rest her head on Reyla's shoulder. Reyla gulped down a surprised breath, her heart skipping. But her rippling excitement brought with it pain and shame. The Frey held strong opinions of same-sex relations, causing Reyla much hurt and confusion. It felt like a betrayal of their friendship and religion every time her heart swelled. How she prayed her heart would change, but its resolve only strengthened with each passing day.

She wished they could stay on the bench together all night, but as the minutes moved on and the air grew cold, she knew it was time to go.

"It's getting rather late," said Reyla gently motioning her head to Arafrey. "How about I wake you up early and we give it another go in the morning?"

Reyla waited for an answer, but one never came. The princess snoozed softly, her breathing quiet and regular.

Reyla inclined her head towards the glowing skies. She supposed Arafrey had pushed herself too hard. The princess was proficient at doing so.

Reyla decided she would leave Arafrey to sleep awhile, feeling selfish for enjoying the closeness. She watched as the moon crossed by the branches of The Life Tree towards the horizon and the fireflies dimmed and returned to their beds.

A soft smile rested upon Reyla's face as she sighed.

Perhaps it really was better this way...

* * *

Treshin Day

Summer Year 3669 – 6BMF

* * *

Judge a mortal, not by the kindness they share with the world,

but by the deeds they keep for themself.

* * *

Tharin Berrin rubbed his face clean. Cold water sprinkled from the shower nozzle in the ceiling, streaming from his caramel-coloured hair onto his lean, green shoulders and down his torso. He scrubbed his arms and over his chest, appeased by the definition appearing from his days of training.

Dalliah's voice called through from the bedroom, "Don't take too long, you're going to use up all the-"

Tharin looked up as the water stopped and drained away. He wrinkled his nose and left the shower to find a towel to mop himself dry.

"Looks like your water's run out." Unabashed and unashamed, Tharin crossed to the bedroom and rubbed the towel over his head. "I always forget your tank's smaller than ours. I'll top it up for you when I get back from my shift."

Dalliah lived in a small grow in Low Town. Unlike Tharin, Dalliah was of common birth and was left with little to her name when her foster parents turfed her from their home at sixteen. It was barely a step up from squalor, but she worked hard to attain it all and refused any hand-outs offered her.

"It's okay, it should rain tonight and save me the job."

Dalliah was pulling the string of her apron as Tharin entered, a white pocketed monstrosity stuck with pins and needles and loaded with threads. They were the tools of her trade as Dalliah worked as a tailor in one of the boutiques on Avenall Road most frequented by noble Frey. She tied the apron over a drab cotton dress with tight sleeves, and drew back her hair with string into a tight ponytail.

"You should get dressed or you'll be late for work." Dalliah passed Tharin his tunic and kissed his cheek.

"Meh, it's only Treshin Day, I'll be on patrol with the rest of the Queen's Guard."

Treshin Day was officially a holiday to celebrate the day their ancestors first settled in Ceynas. Families would gather and hold feasts to celebrate but the festivities at the palace were an altogether privileged affair where the nobles would gather for afternoon tea with their king and queen. The true meaning of the occasion had fallen to the wayside over the last few generations, however, and it was now used to debut the young men and women of Frey nobility looking to wed.

Tharin had no interest in such matters despite being introduced on Treshin Day himself. He was more than contented to continue serving his king and kingdom alongside his friends.

He wrapped his arms around her middle, squeezing until her breasts pressed against his chest. "No one will notice if I'm a few minutes late. We've more than enough time to-"

"As tempting as that offer is, I have a flock of ladies with last-minute alterations to attend." Dalliah kissed his lips. "Will I see you tonight though?"

"Afraid not, my parents should be back today."

Dalliah pressed her lips as she pulled away, her smile gone. Tharin's parents were traditional noble-born Frey who looked down on those of the lower class. Regardless of the history the pair shared, his parents, and indeed the entire upper echelon of Frey society, would be most unwelcoming of his relationship with Dalliah. Even more so than they were his decision to join the military.

"It's just for a little while longer," he promised as Dalliah peeled away. "Once I've got a bed in the barracks they'll have no way to keep tabs on me. Then we can spend as much time as we like together."

Dalliah's features slid sideways having heard his promises many times before. Tharin rubbed the towel over his skin and pulled his tunic over his head.

"No, really. I've already spoken to Captain Valren, I'm just waiting on a bunk to open up."

Dalliah's lips crinkled as she sucked on her thoughts like sour candy. They'd have no need for him to bunk in the barracks if Tharin could just pluck up the courage to tell his parents of their relationship.

She quietly helped Tharin with his shiny wooden arte-formed chest plate and leaf-leather bracers and greaves, tightening the straps to save him from struggling. He then pulled a crimson cape over his shoulders and fastened them to his armour, the pins featuring red dove sigils to show his position on the Queen's Guard.

"Don't work too hard today. I'll try to visit tomorrow," he promised, collecting his sword and shield and leaving for the palace.

The morning sun was still rising over the forest canopy when Tharin arrived at the barracks. Its orange glow beamed through the mystic blue hue of The Life Tree, casting the square military builds in a vibrant green light.

Men from the palace guard huddled in the training yard. Anyone who was not already stationed about the palace that day was called in to manage the festival. They all wore leaf-leather armour with shortswords strapped to their belts, but only those on the royal guard wore capes. Mika and Gurrein were in red like Tharin, but others, like Reyla, wore the green of the Princess Guard.

Captain Valren stood tall among the masses, his long horse-like face set and pre-eminently unamused by the day's antics. "We'll have an extra few hundred bodies in the palace and grounds today, so I need everyone to be on high alert. Keep an eye out for any undesirables hoping to sneak into the stores or pocket themselves a trinket from the palace."

By undesirables, Captain Valren meant common Frey but it seemed not to register with the men among the palace guard. It was as if they considered themselves apart from the lower class simply because they were guards. They acted as if there was somehow a good commoner and a bad one, when they were all equally unwelcome by those lucky enough to be invited to the palace that day.

"I want the base guard in the throne hall and gardens today. Tarrek, take Rambush to the second floor and keep anyone from wandering anywhere they shouldn't." Captain Valren pointed as he handed out orders and men turned to their duties. "Denter, Fenwilt, I want you two on the front gates."

Reyla and Gurrein shared a look of derision at being posted by the gates and sulked away to take their post. The front gates were by far the least desirable of all the postings and Tharin wondered what Gurrein did to be landed with it since he was on the Queen's Guard like Tharin. It was of little surprise Reyla was posted there, however, the higher-ups often picked her for the worst roles as some kind of punishment for being there in the first place.

"The rest of you are on patrol. Ones and twos, and if I catch anyone skiving you'll be busted down to mucking stables. You hear me?"

With his friends stationed elsewhere, Tharin chose to go it alone and wandered in the general direction of the pack toward the palace. The grounds sprang with vibrant flowers as they entered the gardens, lilies mostly as they were the queen's favourites, and birds fluttered overhead. Large floral bouquets of pink roses were placed at the intersection of each path for the festivities and pale-coloured bunting was strung between the posts and trellis.

"You coming down the Hill's tonight," asked Mika, his voice a strong baritone which twanged with a northern accent.

"Nah, I'd better go make nice with the folks tonight. Gods help me if I miss another family dinner."

"I would've thought you'd be spending it with that lass of

yours," Tarrek grinned with his suggestion. "You gonna tell them about her yet, or what?"

Tharin's teeth clenched at the mere suggestion. "Or what. Definitely or what."

Tarrek clapped his hand on Tharin's shoulder and chuckled. "You know, I can never tell if you're brave or dumb."

Mika snorted, "A man can be two things."

"Hey! No fair."

Beyond the garden, the palace was grown. A structure of ancient oaks woven with pine, cedar and burlok, its towers were wrapped in streamers and hung with lanterns beneath the parapets. Tharin left his friends by the rear entrance and followed the garden around to the entrance where Frey were already arriving. They wore long sagely robes in bright colours and doused themselves in perfumes in a strange high-societal war on the senses. While the men commonly wore their hair long and straight, the women dedicated their hair to intricate weaves and plaits sculptured onto their heads. It reminded Tharin of all the times his mother sat by her vanity mirrors while a maid laboured over the long caramel-coloured waves of her hair, but little more. He may have been one of them once, but he no longer felt any love or longing for the thralls offered by noble society.

* * *

Tharin's Treshin Day was uneventful as he circled the palace grounds and back again. He was just rounding the palace to the entrance when he noticed three guards huddled by the bushes.

His brow furrowed upon making his approach. "What're you up to?"

The three guards snapped to attention and hid their hands behind their backs. Tharin recognised them as palace guards, but only knew the middle one by name.

"Oh, it's only you, Berrin. Thought you were Valren."

"Not this time, Horsh."

Horsh was among Tharin's least favourite men on the Palace Guard. He wore no colours, only a permanent look of righteous condemnation which hung off the protrusion of his brow like a primate.

"What you got there?" Tharin lifted his chin to the cloth Horsh was trying to hide.

The two buffoons sniggered as Horsh presented Tharin with a gooey sponge-like substance piled into an old rag. It stunk of rotten eggs and forced Tharin to cover his mouth to avoid recoiling.

"Ugh, what've you got that for?"

"We're gonna sneak down the fence and stick it where Fenwilt's got to deal with it all day." Horsh indicated across to the entrance where Reyla and Gurrein were on duty.

"You what?" Tharin couldn't believe they planned something so cruel, but then Horsh was always picking on Reyla. They all did. They didn't care if she was a decorated war hero or could best them in nearly any match. All they cared about was keeping things the same as they always were, ignorant of the progress to be made with change.

Tharin straightened himself. "You'll do no such thing."

"Is that so?" Horsh scoffed as his cronies fell in to support him.

"I won't let you. Here, give me that!"

Tharin grabbed for the rag but Horsh pulled it away. He ducked under flailing arms as the other two tried to run interference and rammed Horsh with his shield. Horsh cursed as his hand flattened against his chest plate, smearing whatever wretched concoction was in the rag over himself.

"I'll make you pay for that, Berrin."

Horsh drew his sword and swung it at Tharin. Steel clashed as Tharin drew his blade to deflect reflexively, but panicked in the face of three opponents. Goop dripped from the wood of Horsh's chest plate as he and his goons surrounded him.

Tharin chuckled awkwardly. "Come on now, Horsh. You don't want to start a scene on Treshin Day."

"Should've thought about that before getting your drawers all twisted over some bitch pig."

Tharin sucked his teeth and sighed. "You shouldn't have said that."

"Which part?" Horsh twisted his head left and right. "Bitch? Or pig?"

Whatever part of Tharin held his restraint vanished in that instance. He flew forward in a blinding rage, his shield swinging in a full-force uppercut to Horsh's jaw. The guard's chin cracked and his head flew back, sending him hurtling back into the arms of his comrade.

Dazed and missing some teeth, Horsh staggered back to his feet and righted himself. "Get him."

Tharin realised himself in time to turn on his heel and run as the two guards rushed him. His sword unsheathed and his shield bloodied, Tharin crossed the gravelled drive in a blur of motions and coming Frey. He wasn't meaning to run to Reyla for help, but aimed her way regardless, the two guards hot on his heels.

Frey were beginning to notice him running, so the two guards backed off and let him go. Tharin glanced over his shoulder to make sure they were gone before slowing, but forgot about his feet and stumbled. He threw out his arms and staggered forward in an attempt to keep from falling. His sword stuck out as he hurtled forward, unable to stop himself as the blade continued towards a very much unaware Reyla.

"OUCH!"

Reyla lurched forward as the blade sliced through her leggings and into her thigh. She hissed and cursed and pressed her hand to the pooling blood.

"Tharin! What're you playing at?"

"I- I didn't mean to! It was an accident!" Tharin's mouth hung wide, unable to explain the full truth of the matter. He dropped his sword and shield and knelt to help Reyla with her thigh.

"You stabbed me! Why did you stab me?"

"Here, let me." He pushed her hands out of the way and activated his artes. Mana collected from his body into his palm as they activated, a soft white glow coming over his hand. Tharin used his artes to soothe Reyla's flesh and stem the bleeding. He then used it to take hold of the molecules in her body and knit the skin back together. "There, all better. We good?"

"We're good." Reyla shook her head in disbelief. "What are you doing with your sword out anyway?"

Tharin looked back over the entrance to see if Horsh and his cronies were still lurking. He wouldn't tell Reyla what they were planning though.

"Oh, you know, I just thought it would like some fresh air." Tharin's cheek dimples appeared as he forced a smile. "It is Treshin Day, after all."

Reyla rubbed her leg and rolled her eyes. It was a little insulting how readily she accepted this as fact, but Tharin would rather that than the truth. "Just put it away and be glad Valren didn't catch you, you'll have someone's eye out if you're not careful."

"Right." Tharin nodded his head. He re-sheathed his sword and collected his shield before righting himself. "You sure you don't want to go to the temple and get it checked out?"

"It's fine." Reyla waved him off. "I'll ask the princess to take a look when she gets back from the temple. They'll be busy enough today."

"Okay, but you'd better not forget. I'll ask!"

Reyla promised and returned to her post, unaware of all that transpired.

Tharin lingered in the entrance a while after. He lapped the palace, ensuring Horsh stayed far away from Reyla for the rest of the day. It was not the first time, nor would it be the last, but Tharin was assured in his duty as much as he was assured in his decision to keep the truth to himself.

It was the least he could do for his friend.

* * *

The Heart of Knowledge

Autumn Year 3669 - 6 BMF

* * *

I never believed in fate.

The Gods left their children to find their own ways,

but every so often, something would happen

that not even I could deny was destined to be.

* * *

Despite her best efforts, Princess Arafrey was at an age where she could no longer avoid the social aspects of her position. She attended any functions and festivals required of her, but with the passing of her twentieth year, there was one thing she had been avoiding that she could no longer. Something horrible and terrible beyond measure: marriage.

It wasn't so much the act of marriage itself Arafrey had a problem with, more everything she would have to go through before and after doing so. Even if she were to disregard the giant leaps marriage would take towards her becoming queen and high priestess, she still needed to suffer through the tireless dance of courtship, a performance Arafrey had no interest in.

Princess Arafrey grew up reading stories of beautiful princesses who fell in love with a prince so suave it weakened their knees and caused them to faint, yet Arafrey was yet to feel any of that. She had yet to find even the faintest flutter of butterflies and was all but certain they did not exist.

Princess Arafrey feared no man could ever draw her excitement, but for the sake of her kingdom, she was obliged to try.

The cart rattled around her as they continued south to Stillcross where she would be staying with Lord Croist while meeting with various suitors from neighbouring lands. Arafrey wore her travelling clothes, leggings and a loose tunic, nothing fancy, but comfortable and light enough to wrap a robe over once they arrived at their destination. Her moss-green hair was tied above her pointed ears into braids, flashing the single silver piercing on the left – the first of her rebellion.

It was a long and boring journey with many stops at inns and manors, but Arafrey passed the time reading the many tomes on botany and biology her mother packed for her. She was hardly pressed for company either. Keya sat across from her in the carriage, knitting as quietly as ever, and Reyla, who was presently sleeping atop the carriage, guarded Arafrey each evening. Plus nine more guards, two driving the carriage and the rest on horseback, they may as well be having a party when they stopped each evening.

The horses whinnied and bickered as a barrage of hail thunked into the front of the carriage. Or so Arafrey thought.

Keya dropped her knitting and turned to the carriage window as an arrow slit through the curtain. She gaped, the red of her eyes going dark as she turned to Arafrey.

"Princess?"

Staggering breaths shook her body as Arafrey stared at her aide. Stunned beyond action, she was helpless as the front of the carriage gave way and threw Arafrey forward. She cried wordlessly and landed on Keya, her body already growing cold. Arafrey scrambled against the dead weight, trying to find her feet when the carriage door flung open.

Arafrey braced herself, but her heart swept with sudden confidence to the blaze of Reyla's chestnut mane.

"Quick, with me now." Reyla offered her hand to Arafrey and yanked her from the carriage.

Holding tightly to Reyla's hand, Arafrey lifted her free arm over her head as if to protect herself from the arrows zipping through the air. Men and horses lay on the ground in a mess of blood and gore surrounding her broken carriage.

"What's going on?"

Reyla didn't respond. She pulled Arafrey between her guards, allowing them to fall in behind them as she cut towards the treeline. They ran like wild horses through the thicket. Trees became nothing more than passing blurs, changing from oak to fir to pine with each minute they continued.

Arafrey's chest burned, her heart and lungs aching through fear and exhaustion. Her energy failed her as the initial adrenaline wore off and a sudden weakness took hold of her limbs. Reyla turned back as Arafrey's strength waned, a hardness upon her features as her warrior's heart led their retreat.

Arafrey imagined this was the face Reyla wore fleeing Sheya with her father. Fearless determination. Strength. Blazing spirit. There was no doubt in Arafrey's mind this was Reyla's truest form. Even then, Reyla was a warrior, a hero.

She was certainly Arafrey's.

"I need you to trust me," Reyla whispered with no need for an answer. "Hide in this tree and wait for my return. Stay quiet.

Understand?"

Arafrey bobbed her head. There was no one she trusted more.

Reyla linked her hands together, boosting Arafrey into the tree. She pulled off her green travel-cloak and passed it up to Arafrey.

"Cover yourself with this. I'll be back, I promise." Reyla flashed a reassuring smile and Arafrey knew she meant it.

She smiled back and then, Reyla was gone.

* * *

The sun dipped behind the forest canopy, stretching the shadows around her, but still, Arafrey waited, knowing beyond doubt Reyla would return for her.

Arafrey wrapped Reyla's cloak tighter around her body, shivering against the chill in the air. It smelt like Reyla. Like grass and hay and leaf-leather. Like home.

She shirked her juniper lips knowing the secret love she harboured for her dear friend would cause them nothing but harm. The Frey deemed same-sex relations a sin and she was their princess and the only heir to their throne. Arafrey knew this, but couldn't help herself.

She was the one who demanded Reyla's promotion to the Princess Guard after the war, claiming it only fair after she saved the life of their king. It was all lies though and her motivations selfish. Arafrey just wanted a chance, a hope.

Maybe she was imagining it all and she was just a fool living out some misguided fantasy, but she would never know for sure if Reyla were stationed on the other side of Freya. However, regardless of Arafrey's motivations, Reyla was already proving her worth on the Princess Guard.

Was there even a Princess Guard anymore?

When Reyla drew Arafrey from the commotion so many had already fallen. Arafrey's thoughts spiralled as she continued to wait, her emotions strangely numb as she processed the fragmented memory of their escape.

Did anyone survive besides herself and Reyla?

* * *

Arafrey's eyelids began to droop. She didn't have the energy to hold them any longer and her head dipped forward. When something ruffled the bushes.

Energy threw back her head and panic woke her limbs as Arafrey prepared for whoever should appear. She thought perhaps she could dive from the tree and surprise any foes but would be quite useless in the face of true danger. Arafrey set the flat of her shoes against the tree trunk, ready to pounce, but collapsed back into the nook of the tree as Reyla waved up to her.

Reyla climbed in beside Arafrey, her cheeks red and her hair slicked back with sweat. She flashed her trademark smile and wiped her brow.

"It's okay, we should be safe now, they didn't follow us."

Returning the smile, Arafrey shuffled along the tree, allowing Reyla to squeeze in beside her. Static circled Arafrey's stomach as their leggings brushed together and their shoulders pressed. It was cosy and closer than Arafrey had ever been to another person without dancing. A blush covered her cheeks but Reyla was not to notice.

Reyla tilted her head back against the tree trunk. Her eyes seemed to stop blinking as she surveyed their surroundings, absolute in her protection.

"You should rest," Reyla insisted and fussed with the cloak to ensure it wrapped every part of Arafrey.

"What about you?"

"I'll be fine, Princess."

Arafrey huffed and Reyla ignored it, leaving her to sleep, but it was not an easy task. Between the tree branches sticking in her side and the rough bark against her hide, it was most uncomfortable, yet it was Arafrey's thoughts which kept her awake that night. She championed her courage countless times but lost it at the last second, unsure what she planned to do once she summoned it.

Reyla shivered and rubbed her hands, likely thinking Arafrey was sleeping and would not notice. It was cute Reyla tried to keep her appearances up around Arafrey, but ultimately frustrating as it made her intentions all the more difficult to read.

Arafrey nudged Reyla and offered her half of the cloak.

"Please, it's cold," she insisted and hailed victorious as Reyla sighed and moved close to share her warmth.

Arafrey hooked her arm through Reyla's under the guise of saving space and tried in vain to keep her thoughts pure. Her heart and extremities throbbed with her racing fancies despite the shame they marshalled. She didn't care if being close to Reyla was a sin or an insult to the Gods, there was nothing and no one to deter her. Yet her heart grew heavy, resigned to the cold fact this was as close as they could ever be.

Within the close protection of her hero, Arafrey closed her eyes. The resolution of her heart lay all her worries to rest and she slept better that night than ever before.

* * *

Arafrey waited for Reyla to jump down from their perch before finally leaving the safety of their tree. She was numb from the shoulders down and rubbed her limbs awake.

"Which way?" she asked.

Reyla turned over each shoulder. "We should head northeast. Away from the road."

Arafrey followed, but she would have followed Reyla anywhere. They walked in nervous silence at first as Reyla continued to watch over her shoulder, but as the trees changed and the landscape flattened, they dared to believe the worst was now behind them.

"Did you happen to see who it was who attacked us?"

Reyla shook her head. "I was sleeping. They were under

cover most the time."

Tired and forced to walk leagues without breakfast, it riled Arafrey's temper beyond measure. How many died? And for what? For gold and silks? Or was it her they were after?

"This is beyond outrageous. Who in their right mind would attack my convoy? Who even would have a grievance with the Royal Family?"

Arafrey blustered through a mass of conifers blocking her path. She wasn't made for the wilderness and each step further only worked to bolster her anger towards their attackers.

"You know," Arafrey ducked under a branch, "I wouldn't be surprised if it were just bandits who got lucky or perhaps even-"

She lost her words to the sight before her. A giant tree glowing with a mystic blue hue, not unlike The Life Tree in Ceynas, grew in the centre of a clearing, except it appeared to be hollowed out into a building of some kind. A large door and windows grew from the glowing bark at strange intervals. Tall grass swayed beneath it and a stone path ran to the door, calling them closer.

Arafrey hung by the treeline with Reyla in joint awe. Neither had ever seen another tree which glowed with the light of the Manastream, nor had they ever heard of one. By all accounts, it should not be possible, yet the Manastream converged in the atmosphere above them and Arafrey knew she was not dreaming.

Swallowing her apprehensions, Arafrey aimed at the door and Reyla reached for her sword. "Put that away. We don't want to scare them from helping us."

Reyla's brows expressed her disagreement but she held back as Arafrey knocked upon the door. A pair of bright coffee-coloured eyes appeared through the crack, their size magnified by oversized circular glasses. An old Frey woman greeted them with a wide smile, her grey hair twisted into a messy bun so only the points of her ears were showing. She ushered them through the door with enthusiastic courtesy.

"Come in, come in. Suppose you'll be wanting a cup of tea. Least I can do. Take a seat. Take a seat."

The door snapped closed behind them and the old Frey ran to a stove to mount a kettle. Arafrey gaped like a fish out of water, unsure where to look first.

They seemed to have entered a library as bookcases grew from the walls. The library spanned several floors above them and many more below, spiralling around the inside of the tree. Rows and piles of dusty tomes filled every space within sight, except for a small clearing at ground level with a fire and some chairs, which served as a living area.

The old Frey gestured to chairs by the fire and invited them to sit. She passed out tea cups and set in across from Arafrey, peering over her glasses with strange aged wisdom.

"So go on then, which book is it?" The woman's voice crackled on the vowels as it warmed up for the first time in what Arafrey could only presume was a long while.

"Book?" Arafrey's hope of finding sanctuary escaped her, leaving only doubt. Just what had they stumbled upon?

"You came all this way and found this place, you must be here for something."

Arafrey's eyes locked with Reyla's but she appeared equally as confused. Their eyes slid to the old Frey, who chuckled.

"Chloris, Keeper of Knowledge at your service and this," she gestured to the tree surrounding them, "this is the Eternal Library. That is why you are here, is it not?"

"Err... No... We were just trying to make our way home. We're a little lost. You see, our carriage was attacked and we ran into the forest and-"

"Don't worry about being followed, this place is protected by magic. Not just anyone can find it. And to find it by accident..." Chloris pulled at the loose skin around her neck with deep contemplation. "Well... Not to worry. Perhaps this is exactly the place you're supposed to be."

Arafrey was too tired to refute destiny and her stomach growled.

"Perhaps I can offer you ladies something to eat. Please, it would be my honour to host you, Princess. There's spare rooms upstairs and you're welcome to explore the Library in the meantime."

Reyla made to protest but Arafrey was in no rush to return to roughing it through the forest.

"All I ask is you treat the Library with respect. There are tomes and relics from ages past within these walls. Things which are not for playing with." Her brows popped over the circular glasses. "But aside from my bedroom, you're free to explore."

"Thank you, Chloris. I shan't forget the kindness you've shown us."

"Think nothing of it, Princess."

* * *

The initial excitement of exploration carried Arafrey through several floors of research papers, history and fiction, but she prolonged their venture as long as it meant she got to be alone with Reyla. They found journals from previous monarchs from across Alamantra and strange trinkets and tools they could give no name too. It put Arafrey's library in the palace to absolute shame. There must have been a copy of every book ever made or written on their planet.

Other than Chloris' bedroom and a locked door on one of the lower levels, they explored every nook and crevice of the Library until the sun faded and they returned to the seats by the fire. The three of them read of fiction, war and science over sweet honeyed tea and ate baked potatoes with carrots and peas in contented silence, the horrors of the past day as long forgotten as Arafrey's urgency to return home.

Chloris hardly lived a life of luxury and would no doubt benefit from a maid or two, but there was a kind of peace beside the crackling fire which Arafrey had never felt before. At that moment, she wasn't a princess or high priestess-to-be. She was just Ara, a girl in the forest with the one person whom she would be truly lost without.

Arafrey thought it a credit to her hero how they currently fared, but she was growing too weary to give it any voice. She stifled a yawn.

"I think perhaps I should retire."

"You can take any of the rooms. There's space for you to have your own-"

"No," Reyla burst, near dropping her book. "I'll continue my guard if that's all right with you. I'll sleep on the floor if I have to."

This pleased Arafrey to no end, but she wasn't about to admit that aloud.

"There'll be no need for that. There's a sofa in one of the rooms. You can throw a bedsheet over that if you're so determined, but I promise you, your pursuers will never be able to find this place. Countless have tried, kings and queens even, and not one was ever deemed worthy of the knowledge residing here."

Arafrey's eyes narrowed with the growing suspicion there was a lot more going on within the Eternal Library than she held the strength enough to comprehend. Chloris was surely not telling them everything, but neither did she appear disingenuous in any way.

"I don't mind if that's what you want," Arafrey lied. She was certain to cry if Reyla left her. "There's no need for you to hurry though, I would appreciate some time alone."

Arafrey wished them good night and found the bedroom with a sofa. Bookcases lined this room also and the moon shone through the thin scraggly curtains, casting a bright white light across the bed. A sigh eased her shoulders as Arafrey released her facade and allowed her emotions a moment of freedom.

The princess dropped to the lumpy mattress and wept for

her guards and Keya. She cried through confusion, grief and anger. She cried for Reyla and herself. She cried for her aching limbs and her dire circumstances. And then, she cried for no reason at all.

Once all her tears were shed, Arafrey wiped her face clean and returned her facade to its place in preparation for Reyla's arrival. She had no bed clothes, but removed her shoes and leggings, and crawled under the duvet. With her eyes pressed closed, she listened to the natural creaks and groans of the Library and the low sounds of conversation downstairs, her thoughts deafening and despicable.

It wasn't Arafrey's fault her convoy was attacked. Nor was it Arafrey who butchered her guards. She couldn't help that Reyla was the only one to survive and rescue her; they were only doing what they needed to make it home. Although, she could probably help how much she was enjoying their newfound freedom.

Shivers cast goose-flesh over Arafrey's skin when the stairs cracked, announcing Reyla's ascent. She brought no candle and entered noiselessly so as not to disturb Arafrey. Reyla then crossed to the sofa where she began undressing to her base layers.

Arafrey dared herself to peek despite tending to Reyla's injuries countless times before. Taut green stomach muscles flashed as Reyla pulled her body armour over her head and set it aside. She rubbed her shoulder, the old war injury more psychological than it was physical these days, but it still caused her pain.

It had been so long since the pair of them had been alone.

Truly alone, for perhaps the first time since before Reyla left her for the army. There were no aides, guards or family members likely to disturb them. There were no sermons or patients to tend, nor lessons for Arafrey to learn. It was just the two of them.

Arafrey pulled the duvet from her face, her hair an untamed mess which fell to replace it. "Umm... Reyla..."

Reyla stopped mid-removal of her shoes and looked to Arafrey.

"Thank you for... Well... I'm just glad that it's you here, is all."

"Any time, Princess." Reyla returned her reassuring smile, but it would not be enough to settle Arafrey's worries that evening.

Arafrey fought against years of teachings and principles to summon her heart's desire and declare her long-harboured feelings. If ever there was a time for truth, this was it. All she had to do was tell Reyla how she felt, it was that simple. Either Reyla felt the same or she didn't. There was only one way to find out. It was worth the risk, wasn't it? All she was risking was her friendship with the only person on the planet she held any fondness for. That was all.

Arafrey righted herself and tidied the duvet upon her knee. But she couldn't do it.

Arafrey's breath shook from inaction as Reyla sighed and finished setting her gear away for the night. She seemed to fight against her thoughts, her motions hampered as she set her shoes aside and came to sit on the bed beside Arafrey.

Their eyes levelled as Reyla took Arafrey's hand in hers. "You're safe with me, Princess, I promise. I will always protect you."

Arafrey should have felt guilty as Reyla mistook her anxiety for shock or fear, but it only rekindled her desires. Everything Arafrey wanted of a king and husband, kindness, caring and wits, Reyla already held in abundance. Here was a Frey who had proven her dedication countless times over, who put her life on the line for the sake of their kingdom. Reyla was perfect in every way Arafrey could imagine. It made her ache body and soul.

"You would, won't you?"

"With my life."

Reyla smiled, and Arafrey could hold herself back no longer. They didn't need to exchange words, she knew it to be true. She loved Reyla and Reyla loved her. With nothing to stop her, Arafrey drew Reyla's face to hers and swooped in to steal a kiss. Her first kiss.

There was a second where Reyla paused and Arafrey feared she had been too forward. She ruined everything. And then it was gone.

"Princess." That was the only word Reyla managed before their lips joined and their bodies began speaking.

Green limbs swept supple skin and subtle peaks as years of confusion fell into clarity. Arafrey's body sparked with electricity, waves of pleasure consuming her under the gentle conduction of Reyla's firm hands. It was a joy like no other, the symphony of their union setting the wrongs of the universe to right with each legging and tunic they cast aside.

Arafrey didn't care if it was a sin, she coveted every press and stroke of Reyla's naked green body against hers. Her hands lingered over hips, nervous, excited as she dared to guide them further. Static caused Arafrey to quiver alongside her hero as dainty fingers played to Reyla's weakness.

Ecstasy passed between them as Arafrey found her stride. There was no more awkwardness, no worries or doubts. They were no longer a princess and guard but two hearts, two bodies, lost to the throws of passion.

It could have been an hour or a week they spent adrift in their whirlwind of stick and sweat, the bonds of time and existence were nothing to them. Years of missed chances and unspoken truths joined them as one. And when they were done, they fell together with no doubts in their love and affection for one another.

Arafrey snuggled under Reyla's arm, the gentle throb of her exhilaration residing where her thigh wrapped Reyla's.

"What now?" Reyla asked, her thumb stroking across Arafrey's arm as if it had always been doing it.

"I must admit I hadn't thought that far ahead."

Reyla snorted. "This was always as far as I got with my plans as well."

"You made plans?"

"Many, but I'm afraid they all ended one way."

Arafrey pulled away to look Reyla in the eyes but knew the sadness awaiting her there. "It doesn't have to though."

"Princess, I can't tell you how I longed for this, and to know you feel the same is a dream come true. But you have your role. As I have mine."

Arafrey's chest hurt with pain beyond measure. "You would set our hearts aside so I may marry some lord-ling and pop out his fat babies?"

"No. That's not what I meant. You know we could ne-"

"I know you're not willing to try. Perhaps I have no choice in who I must marry but I wasn't aware that dictated who I should love in the meantime." Arafrey rose from the bed in search of her tunic and leggings.

"You'd have us enter a relationship knowing it would have to end?"

"That's better than the alternative, isn't it?" Arafrey returned to the bed, taking Reyla's hands in hers. "Isn't it better we enjoy this while we can? I fear I shall continue to love you regardless, so isn't it better we play pretend and keep this one happiness to ourselves?"

Reyla pulled her hands away. "You can't play pretend forever, Princess. At some point we're going to have to grow up."

"Then let me love you until then. Let me love you until it's time for me to grow up and be queen for our people. That's all I ask."

Tears dripped from Arafrey's chin as she awaited her answer.

"Until it's time to grow up?" Reyla asked.

"Until it's time to grow up," Arafrey confirmed.

Reyla smiled and kissed Arafrey's lips, "That, I can do."

* * *

Whispers On The Wind

Autumn Year 3670 – 5 BMF

* * *

Delicate fingers wrapped around a smooth black stone, their lilac shade glowing with the activation of mana. Ollias used his artes to press and tighten the stone on a molecular level, staring into the open fire beneath a starlit sky.

"What 'chu doing there?" asked Takka, the Chieftain's son. A young Estra, Takka still had the thin horse body of a foal, and a young man's torso grew from the neck to a tan face not dissimilar to his own.

"I'm practising my patience," Ollias replied, his eyes sparkling with the mystic blue of the Manastream in the atmosphere above them. He pushed the stone between his thumb and forefinger to show Takka. "You see, this stone was once a piece of coal deep in the mines of Ruglor, and with patience, you can turn stones into diamonds."

Ollias twisted his hands to deflect as the stone vanished up his sleeve. Takka gaped and marvelled at the petty parlour trick.

"How did you do that?"

Ollias beckoned him closer and whispered in his ear, "Magic."

Catching the air by Takka's ear, Ollias pretended to find something there. A diamond, one no bigger than a bean, now replaced the stone between his thumb and forefinger. Ollias smirked as Takka's eyes grew as wide as his hanging mouth, unsure what to believe.

Ollias placed the diamond in the boy's palm and closed his fingers around it. "You keep this one. Put it in a ring or necklace. Consider it an investment in your future."

Takka's chest puffed with pride and he nodded his head. The Estra were hardly rich and it was likely the first one to ever find its way into Takka's hands. Ollias cocked his head and grinned at the boy.

"Go on. Away with you."

Chieftain Kronso laughed from across the fire. "I should be surprised if my son has not traded your diamond for a spear by week's end."

The Chieftain's horse-legs were folded beneath a solid chestnut body with a thick black tail. His upper torso was built with more muscles than Ollias dared to count for fear of inadequacy, but Kronso was as kind as he was intimidating, once you got to know him. The hair upon his head was as thick as that in his tail and he left it loose to hang over his broad shoulders, where dark tribal tattoos reached over towards his lean pectorals.

"I fear a spear may prove more useful in years to come."

Kronso scoffed. "Always with the doom and gloom. You're a strange one, Outsider. There is no need to be worrying about the future."

"If only I could tell you all there was to worry about."

Ollias would not tell. He would never tell. It was not his place. Despite often wishing it were different, he was tasked only to watch and listen and wait.

"Do your seers not already warn you? Surely Gainan is not too blind to feel the change in the wind."

"It is not for you to worry what our seers predict, my friend."

Oh, but it was, Ollias wanted to tell him. Ollias knew it all. It was his single purpose on Alamantra. His reason for being. Should the worst come to pass and the champions fail, the fate of the planet would fall to him.

Ollias grit his teeth. A high-pitched whine rang through his ears, causing Ollias to wince away from the fire.

"After all I did for her and she's betrayed us." The words slid in Ollias' ear through the Manastream like a poisoned draught.

It was always one voice.

The voice of honey and lies.

Hers.

"She will not oppose me any longer."

Ollias relaxed his eyes and allowed the vision to come, his campfire fading to darkness as a woman appeared within the nothingness. The fabric of her hooded cloak hid her identity on this occasion, but there was only ever one person who appeared before him. She was the reason he was born unto Alamantra. The one who would change the planet to their design.

"Call in your sisters. I want her gone."

Ollias sniffed at the itch prickling his nose.

"Perhaps she's simply unable to respond without giving up her cover," a second voice echoed. He hardly ever knew who they were, but still he listened. It was why he was there. "Don't you think we're rushing to-"

The woman's hand snatched at an invisible object and pulled it close. "Did you think that was a request?"

"No, Mother. Please, I just-"

"You just what?"

Even Ollias could feel the heat from the woman's breath. He swallowed and cast silent prayers for the next moments to go smoother than the last.

There was a sigh Ollias didn't see, and the voice responded. "I shall see it gets done."

The vision faded and Ollias returned to his fire in Estra.

"Where were you just now, Outsider?" asked the Chieftain over their fire.

"I wish I knew." Ollias sniffed and rubbed his nose clear of static.

"I think perhaps you spent too much time in the smoke house. Would you like me to fetch you some water?" The Chieftain chortled with no intention of moving.

The Estra considered Ollias weak, and liked to think their smoke houses would prove too much for him. He tried not to hold it against them. The Estra were not especially keen on outsiders, given their history of Ruglor and Dura carving out their territories from north and south, but Ollias was neither and managed to sway their favour with his artes. Six months they travelled the Estra grasslands together. It was not long, but time enough to soften the walls of Ollias' heart. However, the forging of their friendship was bitter-sweet, for it was their growing bonds which meant Ollias could stay no longer.

"I'll take my leave in the morning and go south. There's something I need to see for myself."

Kronso crossed thick arms across his chest. "You gallop strong and true. You will always be welcome among my clan, Outsider. May Beydos stride by your side."

Ollias stood to walk away and placed his hand upon the Estra's muscular shoulder. "And you, my friend."

Ollias tried to keep moving. He should have left it at that and walked away, but invisible hands seemed to crush his chest and hold him in place. His once cold heart beat across the thousand leagues they travelled together, and not even the Gods could stop the words from escaping his lips.

"Promise me, Kronso. If a star ever shines in Bohet's smile, be sure not to trust it. Ride your people to Ruglor. In the mountains, you will be safe."

Kronso snorted. "I'd have a hard enough time sending my people north, they'd sooner perish than live under some mountain."

"Then they shall perish."

Ollias patted Kronso and continued walking to his tent.

"Ignore me as you wish, my friend. You will know I speak the truth when the ten circle Vespiria."

Chief Kronso remained by the fire for some time after that, alone with his thoughts.

The Outsider was a strange creature but his warning hailed

with far more conviction than any seer. It sent pins and needles down his limbs with a nervous energy which twitched his ears like a coming storm. Was it possible he knew something their seers didn't? Could he see further or clearer than they could?

Kronso collected his thoughts and looked to the stars.

"Bohet…"

He found the constellation for the God of Good Fortune with his chalice to hold the wealth. Bohet had no smile though, just the Manastream passing over the constellation in an ever-changing swirl of mana. Vespiria was not one he had heard in many years and he thought it entirely possible Ollias was just leaving him with one last jibe. Still, Kronso watched the stars and checked Bohet again before he retired to his tent. He looked up before going to bed the next evening, and the one after that, and would continue to do so for years to come...

...Just in case the Outsider was right.

* * *

Crossed Hearts

Winter Year 3670 - 5 BMF

* * *

The physical and spiritual needs of the people of Freya were tended by the priestess and sisters of the temple of each city or village. The examination room of the Ceynas temple was on the ground floor of the two-storey building grown from the roots of The Life Tree. It was a bland and cold room with several cabinets, a counter and an examination table, where Princess Arafrey sat, her legs dangling over the side.

Arafrey presented her arm to her grandmother, the loose sleeve of her robe pulled up to her elbow to expose the soft-green of her skin. Yarafrey pressed icy fingers against Arafrey's wrist and counted her pulse.

Yarafrey was, at least by Arafrey's reckoning, the most dislikable person on the planet. She kept her grey hair in a tight vertical roll at all times, pulling the loose skin of her age back against her angular skull to form a permanent scowl across her face. There was little familiarity between them. Arafrey was soft, graced with comely features and waving hair of moss-green. If not for their green skins and pointed ears, there'd be nothing similar about them at all.

"I told you I'm fine, you don't need to keep checking."

"As long as you remain the last heir of my kingdom I will continue to proceed with caution." Yarafrey snatched her hand away, leaving white imprints from where her fingers dug in too tightly. "Unless of course Elsa has plans to have another child that is. Perhaps a man this time, who can sow his seed and replenish our line."

Arafrey ran her tongue over the back of her teeth to stop the words she wished to say. It mattered not to Yarafrey what trouble her parents had conceiving her in the first place. Nor did it seem to matter how it had been the hubris of her grandparents, uncles and cousins which left Arafrey the only heir.

"Now then, I shall see you next week. Have your aide increase your meals and make sure you eat it all."

Arafrey sighed. "Yes, Grandmother."

"There's nought but skin and bone on you. What man will entrust such narrow hips with their lineage?"

Arafrey looked to the door, knowing Reyla stood on the other side and could likely hear her response. Until they grew up. That's what they promised upon their return from the Eternal Library, yet Reyla had hardly spoken to her since. Although it was unsurprising given their positions. After returning from the Library, the Princess Guard required all new staff and Reyla was forced into the unofficial role of sergeant, at least for the time being. Between her parents' fussing and her grandmother's newfound interest, they hardly found a moment of quiet to appreciate their secret love for each other.

"Have a lovely day, Grandmother."

Arafrey rolled her sleeve back down and jumped off the examination table, the salvation of the corridor only a few steps away.

"And don't forget you're running the sermon tomorrow."

Arafrey's face twisted to withhold her curses. Of all the

things she wished to do, preaching a religion which condemned her love to a fiery damnation ranked among the lowest. She could think of nothing worse, save perhaps a dinner with her Grandmother and the Weiss twins. The thought sent a shiver down her spine.

"I'll see you tomorrow, Grandmother."

* * *

Arafrey drew a deep breath as the door closed behind her.

"Ready?"

Reyla gathered in the corridor, her chestnut mane presently shorn to her chin with a shaggy fringe which covered her hazel eyes. She wore her Princess Guard uniform of cotton and leaf-leather. The green woollen cloak draped over her shoulders was clasped with brass dove sigils to her wooden arte-formed chest plate. The pattern was repeated upon a round wooden shield with a metal rim, which she clasped to her arm, and upon the leaf-leather sheath of the sword hanging from her belt.

"The queen said she would meet you at the palace for dinner," was all Reyla said, the light in her eyes hollow. She had dark rings around her eyes too and her body swayed despite the attempts to make it seem otherwise. Arafrey knew Reyla had been pulling double shifts while waiting for Captain Valren to find replacements, and was likely pushing herself too hard, but this was not the place to press such concerns.

"Then we should return to the palace. Apparently, I've got a sermon to plan."

Arafrey awaited Reyla's cheeky smirk or a stifled laugh, but not even that roused any cheer or teasing. She didn't understand it. Tired or not, they finally expressed their love for each other, everything was falling as it should. Reyla should be happy. Arafrey was. She was happier than she had been in a long time. So why was Reyla so troubled? Did Reyla regret their time together? Did she fall prey to the Frey and their twisted beliefs same-sex relations somehow offended the Gods?

It sent ice through Arafrey's chest. Her once lonely heart trembled at the mere thought of losing what little she fought so hard to attain. If she could just get Reyla alone. If they could talk, carry on where they left off in the forests. If she could just say something, anything. But how to get Reyla alone?

It was her mother who gave Arafrey the idea later that evening at dinner.

Arafrey looked more Elsafrey's child than anyone else's, although Arafrey would never hope to be as effortlessly graceful or refined as her mother. Queen Elsafrey was the embodiment of everything the Frey considered important. She read sermons with passion and care. She tended to her patients with love and unparalleled skill and intelligence. She was invested. Beautiful. Devoted. She was everything Arafrey was not.

"Send Lorelle home. I'm sure Reyla won't mind helping you ready for bed, will she?"

Reyla, stationed by the door across from a guard in the red of the Queen's Guard, bowed her head as if to accept the order.

Arafrey started, her plans setting into motion, and passed the order for her aide to leave out her bedclothes and retire. Her body filled with static and, all of a sudden, she was too weak and too strong in the same breath. She couldn't wait to finish her food and get ready for bed. That was when she would confront Reyla.

"Are you prepared for your sermon tomorrow?" Elsafrey wiped salad dressing from her mouth, the common act somehow made effortlessly fluent in a way Arafrey could never hope to replicate. "Don't pretend like you forgot again. I need you to cover me while I tend to a patient in Low Town."

"Can't I tend the patient and you do the sermon?"

"Not this time." The quiet scorn in the emerald of Elsafrey's eyes ended any hopes Arafrey held of arguing the point further.

What did Arafrey care about sermons anyway? All she needed to do was finish her plate and bid her mother goodnight, then the moment she so desperately needed would be upon her. She would lock the door and wrap her arms around Reyla and take it from there.

Arafrey scooped vegetables into her mouth, the memo of increasing her plate sizes having seemingly made its way to the kitchen staff without her mention. Each carrot, mushroom and pea dropping into her stomach landed like a mighty pulse which echoed through her body. She cleared the plate like a beast starved through winter, the pulse growing, throbbing, urging her forward.

"Careful, Dear, you'll choke."

Arafrey cleared her throat and wiped her mouth clean. "Just making sure I got it all. I wouldn't want Grandmother to think I was trying to lose weight again."

Elsafrey smirked, "If she keeps telling the kitchen staff to increase your portions, we may have to space our evenings out a little more. I'm afraid my body doesn't work as fast as it used to do."

The minutes Elsafrey used to finish her dinner were the most excruciating. Arafrey tried to contain her frustration for fear it would give away her plans before she could enact them, but was unable to stop her foot from tapping. Her excitement doubled as Elsafrey wiped her mouth and set her cutlery aside.

"This was lovely, Mother, but I think I should get started on preparing my sermon if it is to be ready for tomorrow." It was a filthy lie and Arafrey had no intentions of doing any preparations at all. She didn't care. She was willing to do anything.

"Will you be coming down for breakfast in the morning?"

"Um, maybe." Arafrey hadn't thought that far ahead, but what did she care of tomorrow? "I'll see what time I have before the sermon."

"As you will. Good night, Dear."

"Goodnight."

The pulse driving Arafrey now pounded, and she hurried Elsafrey and the guard from her room. She snapped the door shut and dropped the latch. This was it. The chance she had been waiting for. She spun, ready to make her move, but was halted, her libido retreating like a scolded puppy from the ire about Reyla as she set aside her shield and gloves.

Arafrey restrained herself, unable to gauge the silence lingering since her mother's departure. What if she was right?

What if Reyla regretted their time together? What if she only said what Arafrey wanted to hear to keep her safe?

No matter how much she wanted it otherwise, Arafrey decided it best to let Reyla make the first move this time.

She moved before the full length mirror and watched Reyla with weighted patience. Reyla's silence continued, her eyes dull and lifeless as if she were just going through the motions. Arafrey's lips trembled as she fought to hold her tongue. It was excruciating.

Reyla took a clip off the dresser and pulled Arafrey's hair up above her ears and began to delicately unbutton the back of her robes. There were ten buttons.

Arafrey's heart cried out with each fumble of fingers against fabric, willing Reyla to say something, anything.

Nine buttons.

She should say something. Her body lurched with each popping button.

Eight buttons.

Surely anything was better than this terrible silence.

Seven buttons.

"How's the training going?"

Six buttons.

"These new recruits are alright..."

Five.

"They have a long way to go..."

Four.

"We lost a lot of good men that day..."

Three.

"It kinda..."

Two.

"Taints everything."

The final button remained as Reyla froze.

The copper finally dropped, leaving Arafrey to judge herself in the mirror's reflection. What a despicable Frey she was. All this time, she thought Reyla was troubled over their relationship. She saw Reyla's guilt and assumed it was over herself.

"This whole time I thought you were avoiding me." Arafrey took Reyla's hand in hers and held them to her heart. "I saw your guilt but never realised why."

"They all died, Ara. All of them." Reyla clenched her teeth as she spoke. "I was the only one. Again..."

Arafrey stroked Reyla's cheek, brushing chestnut hair behind her pointed ear. "You cannot hold yourself accountable if you succeed where others do not. It was your job to survive and protect me. You did your job, and you did it well."

Tears welled in Arafrey's eyes. Although she knew the men they lost, they were more than just men to Reyla. The army was her home and her comrades, her family. She trained with many of them and together they whiled away many nights of storytelling and sleeping rough. There Arafrey was feeling sorry for herself and all the while she left Reyla tormenting herself. How foolish she was for not seeing it before.

"I don't understand why I keep surviving." There was a sickening softness to Reyla's voice, something akin to a child and not at all the warrior Arafrey knew her to be. "There's nothing special about me. We all trained the same, all wore the same gear and yet I stand here and not them. I can't believe that it's just luck or even fate, it all just seems so..."

Reyla couldn't finish as the words stuck in her chest. She wouldn't shed a tear, but the building emotions turned her skin grey.

There was nothing Arafrey could say to ease Reyla's guilt. How could she, when she felt it too? She squeezed Reyla's hand tightly in hers and kissed her softly on the cheek.

"We honour the lives of those we have lost by living on," she whispered in Reyla's ear. "Your comrades would be happy you survived. As I am."

"I'm glad too," Reyla breathed, her cheeks rouging as their foreheads pressed.

Arafrey's cheeks flushed with endearment. She knew all the many reasons they should have left their feelings in the library but the distance between them was already too much for her to bear. One day Arafrey would have to be queen and high priestess, but for now, she just wanted to be happy. Didn't they deserve that much?

Reyla made her happy. She made her whole. Reyla made her days brighter and her duties bearable. She was the only friend and protector Arafrey would ever need, and all she wanted was to spend as much time together as possible until the day came that she had to become queen and give her life to her people.

Until it's time to grow up, they agreed, holding each other tightly before the mirror.

They would never really be certain whether the knowledge it could end at any time would make their romance more bitter or sweet, but neither was willing to consider the alternative. It wasn't overnight, but they made it work. Their plans often fell through, and moments were interrupted, but in the time they were together, they were happy, and they were at peace, which was all either of them really wanted.

* * *

I guess there are many things which drive a person.

Sometimes it's hate. Often times it's greed or jealousy. But for Princess Arafrey and Reyla Fenwilt it was always love.

Their love for their family and friends. Their love for their kingdom.

Their love for one another.

When you do things for love, as they would soon discover, you find yourself doing things you would never normally consider doing. Things such as possible treason, travelling in underground death-traps or uniting nations to start a war.

But, I'm getting ahead of myself.

* * *

March of the Emperor

Winter Year 3670 - 5 BMF

* * *

Callius Gabris hung off the side of the sofa, sleeping, a puddle of drool where his face squished against the velvet cushion.

A Duran of massive proportions, he was no longer a young man of potential. He was a man, a king, and most tragically of all, a widower left to tend the Duran throne alone.

Callius snorted and stirred from his stupor. Stubble clung to the square of his chin and his cheeks were bruised from lack of sleep as violet eyes opened to the mess of his ready room. He rolled his feet to the floor and pushed himself upright, rubbing his eyes free from sleep.

His mouth ran dry as the desert and his head pounded like the hooves of a thousand warhorses. Callius didn't remember making it to his bedroom, nor did he remember where he was drinking, but it mattered not. He was awake. The world was cruel and grey. And she was not there.

Fully nude, Callius rose from the sofa, his body lean and tan. His joints cracked and his muscles strained through fatigue and malnourishment, but their cries were ignored. Instead, Callius grabbed an open wine bottle from the table and gulped the contents, all the while staggering across the room to the open window.

The morning light had yet to reach the view of the palace gardens from his ready room. Frost covered the wooden trellis and empty flowerbeds, the flowers gone and waiting for spring.

Shadows hung from the veranda and steam rose from the bathhouse windows, serene despite his growing malady.

A click and creak announced the entrance of someone.

"Ah, Your Highness. You're awake." Mattu was Callius' current page and he didn't turn to greet him. "Would you like me to fetch you some breakfast?"

"Just fresh clothes."

"Yes, Sir."

Callius swayed. His eyelids flickered as his eyes readied to roll. There was nothing Callius could think of more monotonous than setting about the daily labours of ruling, but despite his wishing, he had little else to do.

He waited for Mattu to leave before draining the last of his wine and staggering to his bedroom. Callius set the bottle on the side as he passed and sighed.

It was going to be yet another long day.

* * *

Callius found his way to his office on the ground floor of the palace and set about his daily notices.

The king's office was one of a number of official rooms held in the palace. His council held the large room next door and there were smaller offices for the master of coin and the captain of the Palace Guard among others, but his was the largest and the only one furnished with a desk and chair as grand as his.

Callius hunched over his notices and chewed his lip as if it would draw his eyes into focus. Not that there was anything in them to interest him. He didn't know why he bothered reading them anymore. Each day brought him the same notices of death, crime and request, but he had long grown numb to their quandary.

What did he care for the struggles of the common man? Or passing of lands from father to son? Why should he spare a thought for those robbed and wronged, when the Gods already stole everything he ever loved and held dear?

His cousin, Tidus Gabris rapped on the door sometime mid-morning and closed the door behind him. Blond hair curtained his pointed cheeks, dimples appearing as Tidus smiled.

"You not attending the council meeting today, Cousin?"

Callius grunted. "If they need me, they know where I am."

Tidus pursed his lips but said nothing, his eyes flicking over Callius to assess his mood. Of all the Gabris extended family, Tidus was the most intuitive and trustworthy, but could never be tied down to a desk. Instead, Tidus worked as captain, commander and right-hand man, jumping between role and post where needed the most.

"I thought perhaps we could get some training in today. Maybe grab something to eat at the tavern after, like old times."

"Why bother with a tavern when we have a kitchen here in the palace?" Callius shook his head at the notion.

"We've always had a kitchen, that's never stopped us before. Come on, let us leave the palace and make like we're young men again. We can drink and sing and dance and chase-"

Tidus stopped himself from saying any more, his true intentions slipping through.

Callius returned to his work and pretended not to hear him. "Not today, I have work to do."

"Fine, but I plan to visit the bathhouse later. I would like it if you joined me."

"I'll think about it," said Callius, but they both knew his promise rang hollow.

Tidus went to press it further, but Callius was saved by the entrance of Julius, their cousin who ran his council.

"If you could just sign off on these, I can have them sent out and we're done for today." Julius hid his true feelings behind a wide, toothy smile. He wore a white toga but layered it with golden chains which clinked as he presented a stack of papers so big it required both hands.

"Just take the seal and press it yourself. Isn't the point of a small council for the king to delegate?" Callius flung the stamp across the desk, forcing Julius to catch it between chest and paper. He had no interest in tending to these menial affairs. Nothing mattered to him now, not gold, not power, and especially not politics. "If you're incapable of making decisions, perhaps I should find someone who can."

"No need, Your Grace. Consider it delegated." Julius bowed and left, the door creaking closed behind him.

Tidus remained, the judgement upon his face as clear as crystals. "Are you sure you want to give Julius more responsibilities? He's already gaining popularity with the council."

"It's his job to gain favour with the council."

"You're a fool to think he lacks ambition. Who do you think should take your place when you fall? Don't you see the vultures circling?"

"You think he plans to usurp me?" Callius scoffed. "I'd like to see him try."

"You continue this path, cousin, he won't have to try."

"You want to bet?" Callius puffed his chest to the challenge.

"Sure. I'd give you a hundred gold if you could swing your sword without vomiting the vineyard you drained last night." Tidus tensed as Callius pushed to his feet.

"You wish to try me, cousin?" Callius kept his hands on the desk to take his weight.

"Please, Callius. I- I don't mean to shame you." Tidus held his hands up. "I would like nothing better than to leave you to your grief, but you're not yourself. You're wasting away."

"And who are you to tell me who I am?"

"Your cousin and oldest friend," Tidus offered to a heart of stone. His eyes dropped and he sucked his teeth. "But apparently that's not enough."

The disappointment and pain on Tidus' face did nothing to sway the king's heart as he turned and left.

Callius sighed and dropped back to his chair. He reached for the bottom drawer of his desk and removed a glass and brandy bottle. Hoping to douse his insult and fury, he poured a generous measure and replaced the bottle in the drawer.

The brandy didn't register against his tastebuds as Callius drank, they, like his heart, felt nothing. There was no food nor alcohol to fill the hole Marella once filled. His queen. His wife. The woman who carried his child to her demise.

Callius necked the remaining brandy in one. His wife and child gone in one fell swoop. It was as if his life were all just some beautiful dream, then one day, he woke up, blinked and they were gone. It was a fate too cruel, and the broken king would do anything to go back and keep dreaming.

* * *

Callius slunk from his office after lunch, venturing to the wine cellar for a strong vintage. He carried the bottle to his suite by the neck like a hunted fowl, stalking the long corridors with a face of thunder to deter anyone planning to get in his way.

Callius pushed into his bedroom and dropped the latch. Wine bottle in hand, he popped the cork and loosened his toga, the linen hanging freely from his gargantuan shoulders.

The room was empty aside from a mattress and a leather armchair made extra tall and wide to accommodate him. Callius ordered the palace staff to remove everything which reminded him of Marella, except they forgot to remove the portrait from above the fireplace.

Drinking wine from the bottle, Callius flopped into the armchair and stared up at his queen. She smiled through the paint beside him, each wearing their wedding clothes the portrait was commissioned to commemorate. Marella was wrapped in white silks and satins, while he was adorned in his finest armour and largest cape. Callius thought himself lucky that day. Marrying the woman he loved and looking forward to a long and happy life together.

Another swig and a gulp.

What a fool he was.

* * *

Callius awoke in a sudden panic.

Sweat dripping from his brow, he scrambled through the darkness to the chamber pot. Wine and brandy returned with a vengeance, retching the air from his lungs on its way to the bowl. He spluttered and rubbed his mouth across the back of his hand, but barely caught air before hurling his head forward again.

Callius struggled against the weight of his eyelids, his chin dipping as he fought the urge to collapse over the chamber pot. He coughed, unable to laugh at his pathetic state.

Drowning in his own vomit wasn't the worst way to go. It wasn't the heroic battle he once hoped to see, but it was better than continuing as he was. Better than living without his love.

"I'm disappointed," an ethereal voice echoed around him. "We thought you were the one to change Alamantra, but you're not fit to run a parade, never mind a planet."

Callius blinked and looked up. A pair of eyes levelled with

his, smooth and grey, like pale stones washed against a sea of flowing silvery hair. He raised a hand to shield his eyes from the white glow of the creature they belonged to, his vision too blurry to catch on anything else.

"Wres you rem umble ugh?" It wasn't what Callius wanted to say, but he was incapable of anything further.

"How pitiful you are," the creature mocked. "Is this how you want them to remember you? The king of piss and sick?"

The creature appeared to triple, double, and then returned to just one, waves of light lingering upon the air. No, Callius wanted to tell it, he didn't want it to end like this, but it was living he could no longer face. What was the point of his suffering? Why should he endure the many labours of ruling and soul-crushing meetings? The politics, the brown-nosing and bookkeeping. What was the point of any of it, if not for his queen and heir?

"What if I told you, the Gods have plans for you, Callius Gabris? What if this was merely the first step on your path to greatness?"

Callius didn't believe it. He couldn't. There was nothing left for him in this world.

Soft, gentle fingers brushed his cheeks and the creature held his face, their touch warm. Soothing. Their warmth spread through his cheeks, circling through his veins like a potent elixir. His lip trembled, unable to put his thoughts into words.

"I promise you this, Callius, child of Zorum, King of Dura, you will gain everything you wish for and more when Alamantra is yours. But heed my warning, king of broken hearts..."

The creature pressed their lips to his.

"You will find no happiness until you do."

* * *

THUMP. THUMP. THUMP.

Callius stirred on the floor, his head spinning.

THUMP. THUMP. THUMP.

"Callius? Can you open the door?" The voice was no more than muffles in the distance to him.

THUMP. THUMP. THUMP.

Callius rolled to his side and crawled to the chair. He pushed to his feet and dawdled to the door in a daze. Swaying, Callius fumbled with the latch and allowed the door to swing past him.

Tidus and Mattu frowned back from the ready room, their faces red.

"Cousin," Tidus breathed with massive relief. "Are you well?"

Callius looked about him, assessing his situation. He was confused and sore from sleeping on the floor, but was he well? A newborn fire crackled deep in his belly as if to answer his inquiry, the words of his mysterious visitor riling his long-lost determination.

"Call the banners," he told Tidus. "I want every man from Labellum to Crova trained and ready to march."

"March? Where?"

Callius held Tidus by the shoulder and pulled him close, "Everywhere."

Releasing his cousin, Callius returned to his room with open arms.

"We're going to raise the grandest army Alamantra has ever seen. Then we're going to march and we're not going to stop until the entire planet hails united beneath one glorious banner…"

The morning sun beamed upon Callius as he turned to Tidus, the planets aligning with his grinning declaration.

"Mine."

* * *

Perfectly Perfect

Autumn Year 3671 - 4 BMF

* * *

With the Empire's army marching in the east,

I often returned my sights to Freya,

if only to remember what it was I'm here to protect.

* * *

Princess Arafrey lay listlessly beneath her duvet. The bedroom door opened and closed. Footsteps crossed the wooden floor and the curtains whooshed open.

"Morning, Princess."

Arafrey grumbled from beneath her duvet. She had never been an early riser, but waking was an insurmountable task that morning.

It was autumn, and she had been working long hours in the temple, treating and healing all the Frey of Ceynas. The changing of the seasons always affected the elderly and those with allergies, so there was more to do than normal. It was stressful but rewarding work, however, the long hours were taking their toll and she was starting to feel the strain.

Arafrey was woken by Ceal, the only Frey willing to join the Princess' personal staff after the tragic loss of yet another aide. The efforts were in vain as Arafrey rolled over and pulled the covers tight over her head before slipping back to sleep.

The second wake-up call was less pleasant.

Arafrey's body twisted to the light in a tangle of moss-green hair and a cream nightdress. The covers whipped away and a large bundle of clothes were thrown into her face. She jolted upright, ready to scold Ceal, only to find the shaggy chestnut mane and hazel eyes of Reyla, her guard.

Arafrey squinted her eyes with added confusion. Reyla was not in her usual guard uniform, instead she was wearing a light leaf-leather armour, a travel cloak and a big grin.

"Get dressed," she said. "We're off out."

Arafrey rubbed the sleep from her eyes. "I thought Mika was working today."

"He was, but Her Grace told me you had a day off. So I had him switch shifts."

Reyla beamed, her smile making Arafrey melt inside.

Reyla had several smiles. For her reassuring smile she would look you dead in the eye and only the left side of her mouth would peak. A true smile, when she was really happy, her eyes would close slowly and her cheeks would tighten but only the very corners of her mouth would move as she took in her moment of happiness. These were less often and harder to spot. Then there was the 'you're stupid but I love you' smile, where her lips would part as she stifled a laugh showing a small glint of her teeth. However, this one, a wide toothy grin accompanied by glistening eyes, suggested Reyla was up to something, something exciting.

The aches and fatigue Arafrey awoke to faded, replaced with a grin of her own as she rushed to get dressed.

Reyla brought her leggings and a beige linen blazer which she wrapped with a leaf-leather belt. She pulled green leaf-leather boots from the wardrobe and Reyla tied them as Ceal pleated Arafrey's hair. Ready for their excursion, Arafrey hardly looked like herself anymore, but could not deny her comfort.

What were they doing? Where were they going? Reyla wouldn't tell her and gave no hints as they left the palace. She led them through the palace gardens to the stables where two horses awaited them. Each was already saddled and readied with saddle bags filled with additional mysteries.

Arafrey's horse was a Frey Whisp. These horses had crisp white coats with green hues, and its mane ran to its knees in glossy waves of moss-green not so dissimilar to Arafrey's. They were considered a rarity and reserved for royalty and knights only. It seemed to shine beside Reyla's horse, which was a murky brown with a black mane. It was a grand horse to be sure, but anything would seem inferior when saddled beside the Whisp.

Atop their horses, they sauntered through Ceynas, west to the outskirts and into the forest. Reyla held her silence and held her horse at a distance within the capital. They were always careful not to show affection for risk of being found out, but as they went along the forest path, their horses leaned closer and closer, until they trotted side by side.

"So where are we going?"

"Anywhere you want, Princess."

Reyla reined in her horse as she swerved to avoid a low hanging tree branch. Trees reached overhead, their colours neither fully green nor brown. Berries filled the bushes on either side of their path where birds chimed sweet blessings between the bushels.

"We have the whole day and nothing to do."

Arafrey smiled, contented. "Nothing sounds nice."

"Then nothing we'll do."

They carried along the forest path to a field of wild lavender flowers which clung to their colour in defiance of the changing seasons. A river forced the path to turn, but they continued off-road to an old oak tree. Shrubs circled the side of the oak tree facing the lavender, but the side facing the river lay bare, creating the natural barrier of their favourite hideaway.

An orange sun glittered over the water as Reyla dismounted and tied up the horses. She held a hand out for Arafrey to dismount, and released the saddlebags to the floor. Together, they spread the blanket on the grass and Reyla delved into the saddlebags, producing various containers of fruit and grape juice.

As they sat on the ground talking about nothing important, Arafrey sighed. The tension residing in her shoulders released and, for the first time in weeks, she eased enough to relax. "I needed this. Thank you."

Reyla just smiled. She would never accept compliments well, but Arafrey felt it worth noting regardless. Without saying anything, Reyla had known she was stressed and arranged a distraction. More than that, they were in the forest, together and alone.

"This is perfect," she told Reyla, "You're perfect."

Again, Reyla smiled.

They finished the fruit and spent a while laying upon the blanket together, watching the clouds. As children, they would throw themselves down on any old patch of grass and spread their arms and legs out as wide as they could, but now Arafrey rested her head on Reyla's chest with a loving arm wrapped around her while idly flirting with their toes.

Arafrey hated how little time she got to spend with Reyla, but she was determined to make the best of any time she could take. Should anyone ever discover their affair there would be dire political and social repercussions, which could affect the entire kingdom, but Arafrey was already on uncertain grounds with her position. She half hoped someone would discover them. At least then she would have an excuse to decline her inheritance.

"What if we didn't go back? What if we left, right now, and never turn back?" Arafrey was only joking but regretted saying it instantly.

Reyla's chest sank from the weight of her thoughts. She swallowed and tightened her hold around Arafrey, hugging her close and kissing the top of her head gently.

Arafrey didn't expect a response after that. There were many things which were just too painful and were often left unsaid. Even when their relationship was still in its infancy, the end was always in sight, and so they agreed early on to just not talk about it – not seriously anyway.

"Where would we go?" Reyla's thumb stroked Arafrey's arm in a soft habitual motion.

"I hear Sudra's nice this time of year. We could start there, maybe go to Askana for the summer."

"You wouldn't want to settle down somewhere?"

"Like you could settle down. You're getting itchy feet just sitting here."

Arafrey chuckled. It was true though; Reyla had never been very good at sitting still. She thought it was likely why Reyla excelled as a maid and soldier. Always ready and raring to go, breaks were for thinking and planning, she would sleep when she was dead. Alert and prepared for any danger. Arafrey could imagine her no different.

She dreamt perhaps Reyla could one day lead her army as a commander or by becoming a knight of the King's Guard. It would mean serving under the king Arafrey would someday marry, but she hoped the endless supply of troops to manage would be more than enough to keep Reyla occupied. It was an entirely selfish dream, of that Arafrey was fully aware, but she held no doubt Reyla would naturally make an excellent knight, and she would dream any dream which didn't end with them parting.

Arafrey willed her thoughts to stray from their path, but it was no good. Doubts flooded her thoughts, the acknowledgement of her selfish dream eroding the sanctity of their hiding place.

It was all well and good now while they were able to sneak away together but what would happen when she got married and had children? Would Reyla still be happy to live a life so ordinary without all the excitement of sneaking around? Reyla wasn't the kind of Frey to consider conducting a true love affair, and nor was Arafrey bound to ask her; Reyla's honour was one of the reasons Arafrey loved her so. Their situation was hopeless, so hopeless it hurt and forced tears to her eyes.

"Why don't we? Why don't we just go? Right now?" She was serious this time.

"We could." Reyla drew a deep, contemplative breath. "We could leave now and live happy lives for a time. But you'd have to leave the forest and watch as your kingdom is run by another. My Princess, I would steal you away in an instant if I thought it would make you happy, but how could I live with myself knowing I was the reason you would never become high priestess? The reason you sat worrying about your people from afar."

She squeezed Arafrey in lieu of her reassuring smile.

"You may not yet see it, but everyone else in Freya sees the queen you'll be one day. Who am I to stop that?"

Arafrey bit her bottom lip as it trembled. She didn't realise Reyla gave their position so much thought.

"Princess, I know our time together is limited, and I know it's selfish of me to want more., but one day you will be queen. You will be high priestess and I'll be by your side, that is how it will always be," Reyla kissed the top of Arafrey's hair. "Even if we can't be together, I will always protect you."

Arafrey turned in Reyla's arms, more assured in her love than ever before.

It was no sonnet, but those five words replaced the three words they would never speak aloud, it was too painful. Five words to give Arafrey comfort and make her warm and fuzzy inside. Five words to make all her troubles fade away and let her know everything was going to work out just fine.

Of course, Arafrey wished to say those three words too, but

instead she smiled and declared:

"You're perfect."

* * *

The Impetuous Peardish

Summer, Year 3672 - 3 BMF

* * *

There were few things on Alamantra Princess Arafrey loved as much as she did Reyla Fenwilt.

Her hero, her warrior, Reyla served as the perfect guard, devout in any task set upon her. A blaze of chestnut hair flamed beyond her pointed ears, the olivine green of her skin contrasting against the silver rings in her earlobes. Her hazel eyes remained sharp and ever alert in her task, even when forced to wear robes and dresses from Arafrey's wardrobe, as she did this evening. Her arms bulked against the sleeves of the navy robes but the fabric hung off her shoulders over her lean frame. Reyla shook her head in the mirror.

"I look ridiculous."

"You're perfect," Arafrey corrected, lips of juniper kissing the green of Reyla's cheek.

After her convoy was attacked, Arafrey refused to attend social functions until her parents agreed to let Reyla chaperone her. At first, Reyla was allowed to attend in her guard uniform, but it deterred people from talking to Arafrey and her parents would only allow it to continue if Reyla dressed more appropriately. Elsafrey then arranged for Reyla to have a nice dress, a bath and her hair washed, but it only muted the root cause.

Despite her military record, the Ceynas nobles could almost smell the commoner in Reyla's blood. Reyla was resolute in her acceptance of their bigotry, believing it a mere fact of life, and followed Arafrey like a dutiful hound as she made her rounds. She never spoke a word, but even so, the Ceynas nobles deemed her less than themselves and never extended the respect Reyla deserved.

Arafrey despised them for it. She resented everything about the so-called noble elite of Freya. Everything from their snobbish fancies and indulgent lifestyles to their treatment of those unlucky enough to be born outside of their graces. Their treatment of Reyla was, however, a good test of those wishing to gain Arafrey's favour. A man who looked down on his people was no king at all, and Arafrey was determined she would marry no one who could not lead her people with the same kindness they showed their equal.

Reyla peered from the bedroom window to the front of the palace. "We should head down. It looks like folk are arriving already."

Arafrey released a guttural groan. It was the Juliban Ball, an event held by the king and high priestess each year in the palace. Arafrey wore her finest gown, a long banana-yellow robe with brown features which wrapped her slender hips to her knees before flaring out like a fish-tail. Ceal spent hours washing, brushing and pleating Arafrey's hair into an intricate sculpture of moss-green folds. She had no choice but to attend.

"Come on, Princess, it's not that bad."

"I beg to differ."

"At least it's not a dinner. No one will notice if we slip away once the wine starts flowing." Reyla wrapped her arms around Arafrey and kissed the point of her ear. "And I'll be right beside you if anyone too garish starts to annoy you."

Arafrey cupped Reyla's cheek. "My hero."

Reyla smirked and pulled away. Arafrey brushed her skirts and together they left for the ball.

* * *

The foyer was lousy with Frey dressed in their best gowns and robes as Arafrey descended the staircase. Stark green faces with pointed ears turned to her entrance and bowed as she passed.

Arafrey smiled to them, but liked none of them enough to stop. Sir Weisser, the master of coin, lingered by the door in a garish orange robe and engaged with Mr and Mrs Asrich, whose family made a small fortune selling ornate arte-formed clocks. Councilman Peardish lifted the hook of his nose to her, but appeared intent on continuing his conversation with two Frey with accents which twanged on certain consonants, suggesting they were northern Frey. Arafrey passed them all equally but pressed a smile they could believe was meant for them.

Bouquets of purple lilies twined the door to the throne hall, perfuming the air as Arafrey entered. Coloured lanterns hung from the ceiling, their flickering candles casting the hall with soft glow of pinks and yellows, and a harp ran pleasant scales through the ambient chatter. Her parents were seated upon their thrones, their hands held between the throne arms in a rare show of affection. They watched over the ball but had yet to notice her arrival.

"Oh, Ara! There you are!"

Arafrey's body tensed and twisted her features as Lieran Weiss parted the crowds with the shrillness of her voice. The young lady spewed pleasantries at the princess without pausing for an answer, her mouth opened so wide she looked like some starving chick. She was a noble Frey with delusions of personal grandeur, her drab hair and plain features decorated with jewels and makeup to entice unsuspecting men.

Lieran was shadowed by her twin sister Tieran, who matched her in all regards except voice. She was the quieter of the two and only ever spoke in short whispers, assuming Lieran closed her mouth long enough to allow it.

"You know these parties are so woefully boring without you, Ara. We've had to listen to father talk business all night."

Arafrey passed a half-hearted smile. She only tolerated the twins and Lieran's familiarity because their father was a prominent businessman who liked to play politics. There was every chance he could sit on the Ceynas Council someday, and Arafrey held no plans on gaining his ill-wishes.

"Come, I think everyone's in the drawing room," Lieran announced, leading them as if it were her duty.

Arafrey allowed it if only to pass sly glances back to Reyla, who was turned seemingly invisible with the arrival of the twins.

The drawing room seated a collection of younger Frey nobles. The sons and daughters of politicians, businessmen and socialites who would one day become the decision makers of Freya. They noticed as Arafrey entered and there was a lull in the conversation, but none raised to greet her.

Lieran and Tieran left Arafrey to find seats among the rabble. They likely hoped to find their husbands and had no further use for Arafrey now they had made their grand entrance. Arafrey held no such hopes. Her only goal was to make it through the evening without causing any trouble and retire as soon as their guests began leaving.

Arafrey caught a passing server and collected a glass of wine. She didn't enjoy wine all that much, but found drinking a great excuse to hold her response or leave when her glass ran empty. It was a tried and tested technique she developed over the years to survive the rigmarole of Frey social delicacies, but it was sadly ineffective against the most egotistical of Frey.

"You'd love the work we've been doing over in Wayforte," Wallis Peardish told her, his arm high above him as he leaned upon the wall as if to tower over her. "Planning for the temple renovations was tiresome, but I think you'll agree it's growing to be a true work of art."

Arafrey sipped wine, quietly hoping that would be the end of it. Wallis Peardish was the son of a Ceynas Councilman who thought himself worthy of Arafrey's attention whenever he could manage it. If not for his bigotry and entitlement, Arafrey thought perhaps Wallis could be a handsome man with such chiselled features and piercing blue eyes, but to her, he was appalling.

"Of course renovations are not all we've been doing. Managing trade with the Sudra has been a real task."

Wallis was sent to Wayforte to mentor under Lord Warren, the local governor. Arafrey shared a hope with her mother that the trip would earn him some humility, but Wallis seemed intent on doubling down on everything his status allowed him.

"Dirty creatures they are. Always half naked and asking for hand-outs." Wallis scoffed and flicked the leaf-green lengths of his hair; it was too long to gain any air though and just wobbled like a turkey-neck. "As if they would be paid any better in Sudra. They keep their criminals as slaves, you know?"

Arafrey's jaw cracked audibly from the strain of holding her tongue, and her fingers coiled into a tight fist. A man like Wallis Peardish knew nothing of the suffering of those less fortunate than himself and didn't deserve the responsibilities thrust upon him by way of his father's status. He was nothing but his name and a disgrace to all Frey. Arafrey was just about ready to give Wallis the full force of her thoughts, when Reyla cleared her throat.

"Princess, we're late to see his Majesty." It was a barefaced lie, but a most welcome one as it saved Arafrey from saying anything she may regret.

Arafrey sighed and forced a smile upon her cheeks. "If you'll excuse me, Mr Peardish. Have a wonderful evening."

"Of course, Princess. I shall see you later."

Not if I can help it, she thought.

* * *

With Reyla quiet and close behind her, Arafrey skirted the wall, making sure to keep a firm blockade of Frey between them and her parents.

King Galafrey and High Priestess Elsafrey remained upon their thrones, a mahogany dais raising them above the hall. Her mother looked as effulgent as ever in a dress made in flowing blue fabrics sprinkled with spots to look like duck eggs, but her father made no such efforts, the dark robe he wore likely the same one he wore to work that day. Galafrey maintained the perpetual stone-carved face of his emotions, while Elsafrey beamed and twinkled like some shiny object you'd place in a bird cage.

Arafrey turned her back to the wall as they neared the open doors to the gardens. The harp still sounded among the chatter, but a light drum and clave were now added to the baseline. A lute plucked and strummed a few chords, raising the atmosphere and clearing the hall for dancers.

Dancing was the last thing on Arafrey's mind and being close to a man like Wallis Peardish ranked lowest on her ambitions. She back-stepped over the threshold, watching to make sure no one saw as she and Reyla slipped outside.

The glowing lanterns continued into the gardens and dotted the flowerbeds, yet the whole area glowed with the mystic blue hue of The Life Tree reaching above them. Arafrey's shoulders released as they passed by the lilies and her jaw unclenched as they trailed the path to seclusion, but it wasn't until they reached the pond that Arafrey finally allowed her facade to come loose.

"Call the sisters to bury me, my soul has left my body. I have no more will to live." Arafrey threw herself upon the bench with a cry befitting her conflict and melodrama.

"Really? And here's me thinking I'd be irresistible in this

robe of yours." Reyla gave an overly feminine twirl to flare her sleeves and skirts. "What do you think? Should I wear a dress every day?"

Arafrey returned to her beloved and squeezed their hands together. "I think you'd look beautiful no matter what you wore, although I do think I prefer the uniform."

Reyla blushed, uncomfortable displaying any sort of affection outside the safety of a locked bedroom. They both knew the consequences if anyone should find them out, but Reyla was so awkward Arafrey suspected it was only partially to blame for her stiffness. Still, there were moments when Reyla's true nature took hold, moments when her confidence bloomed and the strength of her heart took the reins. Arafrey thought perhaps Reyla could do anything in those moments, name any task and there would be no doubts to her Reyla would excel, for they were what made Arafrey love Reyla the most of all.

The music changed and a new song played, one Arafrey enjoyed from her childhood. Reyla offered her hand to Arafrey, grinning like they were the only two on the planet as she pulled the princess into a dancing embrace.

"I love this song," said Arafrey, pressing herself against the solid muscle of Reyla's stomach. Her good senses taking their leave with the fall of her facade, Arafrey hardly even realised she was speaking and was unable to stop once she started. "I always imagined it playing at my wedding. Do you ever think about getting married?"

"To you?" There was a weighty pause as Reyla considered it, her words passing in time to the waltz now playing around them. "Sure... Occasionally..."

"Would you wear a dress?"

Reyla snorted. "I've never really thought about it. I guess what I was wearing wasn't that important."

Arafrey's heart squeezed at the thought, but the conversation appeared to be leading into a direction Reyla wasn't overly keen on. She spun Arafrey and stepped away, retreating into the shadows.

"Oh, Princess there you are," came a voice.

Arafrey started in the face of Wallis Peardish. Her heart skipped beats as she tried to gauge how much he had seen. All the while Reyla remained in the shadows, silent, tense.

Was their secret out?

"I was looking for you in the party," offered Wallis, his palms wide as he moved towards her. "It's really not the same without you."

"I just stepped out for some air, Mr Peardish. Thank you for your concern though."

Arafrey tensed as he entered her personal space.

"I'm glad I caught you alone, Princess. I feel I can be frank with you," his noble entitlement lifted his tone with his nose. "As you are no doubt aware, I am the most eligible bachelor in the whole of Freya. My father sits on the council and is the richest in Ceynas, his businesses profitable, our connections endless."

As he spoke, he drew in closer and closer. His hands waved as he listed all the ways his family were blessed. Arafrey stepped back, but he snatched at her hand, pulling her close. Panic jolted through her senses like a rabbit caught before a fox, but she was unable to break loose.

"Let's stop these foolish games and cut to the chase." His arm coiled around her waist. "You know I'm the only one suitable enough to become king. So how about it, Princess? What do you say?"

"I have a few thoughts-"

THACK

Reyla descended from the shadows and punched him straight in the face. Wallis recoiled, blood spraying from his nose as Reyla placed herself between them.

"How dare you!" Wallis yelled grabbing his face and running back into the party crying, "Guards! FATHER!"

Arafrey wrapped her hands around Reyla's arm and pressed in close.

"Are you alright, Princess?"

"Yes, thank you. Though you probably shouldn't have punched him."

"Worth it," Reyla snorted. She winked before leading them back into the party where a crowd already gathered.

"What is the meaning of this?" Councilman Peardish huffed towards them, his face purple with rage. "How dare you assault my son? Guards, arrest her."

The music stopped and Frey huddled to see what was going on. Murmurs lapped the throne hall but were too many and too quiet for Arafrey to hear.

Arafrey raised to meet the guards rushing from the entrance and doors. She would not allow Reyla to be arrested and tried to stand between them.

"It's okay, Princess," was all Reyla said, before bowing her head and presenting her arms to the guards.

Arafrey hoped the guards would not notice it was Reyla they had come to arrest, but Tharin was among their ranks and they all quickly fell to smirks and amusement.

"What are you waiting for?" the councilman flamed. "Arrest her!"

"Look Father, she hit me!"

The guards looked at Arafrey in confusion. They knew as well as her Reyla would never do anything without reason, and no doubt suspected Wallis deserved anything coming to him.

"I'll have you sent to Old Wood for this!" the councilman yelled, but Reyla remained silent, her eyes to the floor.

By this time King Galafrey and Queen Elsafrey had left their thrones and pushed through the crowd.

The councilman turned to them. "Your Grace, I applaud your efforts with those less fortunate than ourselves, but to invite this kind of brutishness into such an event is unfathomable. Do what you like, you can give it a dress and put on make-up and perfume, but at the end of the day a pig is still a pig."

Arafrey's fury soared as Reyla sunk further into herself. Although the slur was common among the nobles, it still soured Arafrey's stomach whenever they used it, but Arafrey was forced to hold her scorn in the face of her parents.

"Did you do as he says and assault his son?" asked Galafrey, the monotone of his voice giving nothing away as his solid mahogany gaze set upon Reyla.

"Yes, Your Grace," Reyla replied.

Arafrey scowled. She didn't even try to defend her actions. Why?

Arafrey tried to interject on Reyla's behalf as Wallis retold his version of the events, but no one paid her any attention. Not even her mother glanced to Arafrey and she was left to watch and fume as Reyla was escorted away to the cells.

A rage unlike any other bubbled in Arafrey's chest. Her teeth gritted and knuckles white, she glared at her parents, unable to stomach the apologies and promises they passed in compensation. She wanted to scream the palace down and call out the injustice so loud the Gods would rise from the grave to beg she stopped.

Reyla, her love, her hero, her champion. What would happen to her now?

Galafrey peeled away with Councilman Peardish as a carriage arrived to take Wallis home early. Arafrey had thoughts to follow him and give him a piece of her mind, but she was stopped as her mother hooked her gently by the arm.

"This way, Dear. I think we've had enough excitement for one evening."

"I don't understand. You know what a horrible sleaze that man is," Arafrey insisted, she didn't care who heard them. "Reyla was protecting me from him."

"She still is. Don't you see?" Elsafrey patted Arafrey's arm and led her through the palace. "The Peardish family are well connected and formidable adversaries. They're also pompous zealots who would think nothing of having someone wrongfully imprisoned. To them, Reyla is insignificant and unworthy of merit. They've likely already forgotten her. But now imagine if she kicked up a fuss. They would make life unbearable for her whenever they could and see to it she ends up in Old Wood."

Arafrey's nostrils flared. She understood the logic but had no plans to let this go while Reyla remained imprisoned.

"But why not just call him out? Why put up with them at all?"

"We must be accepting of all our people and all their faults. At least on the surface," Elsafrey winked and waved her arm. "Oh guard? Guard? Would you please escort my daughter to her room?"

Arafrey sulked, powerless to stop Reyla from spending the evening in jail. It wasn't fair. It was all so strange. It was also rather curious her mother didn't know the name of this guard she called. By her reckoning, Queen Elsafrey must have known all the palace staff and their extended family by name, if not the whole of Ceynas.

Reyla stomped and lifted her shield to attention. "Yes, Your Grace."

Arafrey's features softened as quickly as they spun.

"My daughter is to remain in her room until morning. Understand?"

"I'll see to it." Reyla bowed.

"Excellent." Elsafrey waved and returned to the party with an air of smug satisfaction. "Good night, Dear."

Arafrey wasn't happy with the way things went, but couldn't deny the results. It didn't make everything all right, but it was certainly better than returning to the party with her mother.

"Right, Princess, you heard her," Reyla's brows wriggled with a devilish suggestion, "I'm under orders to march you to your room and put you to bed."

"And if I refuse?" Arafrey pouted her lips.

Reyla cocked her head, her confidence tripled in her uniform. "You know I could just put you over my shoulder, right?"

"Oh dear, that is a tempting offer, but I don't think my parents would appreciate us making another scene. Whatever shall I do?"

Arafrey led them up the servants' stairs to avoid guests, but turned back in the fold in the staircase. She leaned in as if to kiss Reyla, but stopped before their lips could touch. Static ran down Arafrey's legs, the thrill of being naughty whetting her appetite.

"Princess, come on." Reyla glanced over her shoulder, her brows knitting. She could face anything but her fear of exposure. "What if someone sees?"

"Then let them." Arafrey held her position, dancing the fine line between torment and seduction, but it was too much for Reyla.

"Princess, please."

"Not until you promise me you'll never do anything so idiotic ever again." Arafrey's eyes stung as she whispered. She couldn't bear to think what she would do if Reyla had been arrested and carted off to Old Wood.

"I can promise to try." Reyla flashed her reassuring smile with little intent on changing. "If you'd let me, I can certainly promise to make it up to you."

Arafrey sighed away and finished mounting the stairs alone. She then turned back to Reyla with a come-hither pout of her juniper lips. "Then you'd better hurry, you have a lot to make up for before the end of your shift."

Arafrey winked and pranced down the corridor to her bedroom, the fabric of her yellow robe fanning as Reyla gave chase. She spun around the door and beckoned Reyla inside, dropping the latch to their sanctuary.

Arafrey sniggered, "I still can't believe you punched Wallis."

"I'm surprised no one's done it sooner." Reyla grinned, her hands gentle as they traced Arafrey's waist and drew her closer. "Besides, it doesn't matter if it's bandits or smarmy nobles, you know I'll always protect you."

"You're perfect." Arafrey pressed her lips to Reyla's, more assured in her love than ever before. She then pulled away ever so slightly, running her tongue over her bottom lip with seductive intent.

"Now… There was some mention before about putting me to bed…"

* * *

The Guardian

Spring Year 4220 – 546AMF

Present Day

* * *

I wasn't there when the universe began.

I was not yet made when the Gods of Creation danced in the darkness of the universe and gave it light and life as a token of their affection for one another. Khora created planets so that Miera may have a place to call home. In return, Miera gave Khora a sun and stars so their life may always have light. Together they gave life to the nothingness that was once a void.

We Guardians came much later.

The Guardians were created to fill a gap in the workforce as the Gods' creation continued to expand.

I was there when Alamantra was born, however. I saw as the Manastream burst from its core and wrapped the planet with five interlacing rings of mystic-blue power. It glistened among the stars with an endless potential even the Gods could not deny.

Miera grew fond of the planet and spent years trying to duplicate its creation with no success. Fearing the planet would grow lonely in her absence, Miera called upon her children to settle upon Alamantra and begin new lives in the mortal realm.

Upon their descent, I became their Guardian.

I lean back against the cushion of my chair and adjust the dial set into the arm. Before me, a great window looks out over

Alamantra. The vision moves with each turn of the dial, zooming in through the atmosphere to the skies above a vibrant forest. This land was once called Freya, but it lost its name when the continent changed. Everything still springs with the life and vibrancy of ages past, but it was never quite the same after the Manafall.

I stop my viewing pane from venturing any further, focusing in upon a tree set among a field of tall yellow grass. The tree's bark cracks and trembles as a faint light breaks from its core. It shakes against the strain, groaning as a giant air pocket appears from its centre. The pocket bulges from the tree like a pregnant belly, forcing it forward.

I squint my eyes. This isn't the first time I've witnessed the birth of a Child of the Manastream, but I can look away no less. An opening pops the bulbous core, light and placenta burst from the seams ripping them further.

The fragile skin of the sack finally gives way and drops the rest of its bounty to the forest. A child flops to the ground, one with lavender skin, two points on her ears and coppery hair. The birthing ooze evaporates from her skin as she flails and scrambles to her feet.

She wobbles and stumbles like a calf finding its way, naked and alone.

I tap my fingers upon the dial, content the end is almost in sight.

How many years has it been now? Four? Five-hundred years? And still the Gods refuse to answer my call. It's enough to make a Guardian question if the Gods read my messages before choosing to ignore them, or worse, are unable to receive my messages at all.

I watch over the child as she leaves to find her destiny. Children of the Manastream were once common on Alamantra, but became a rarity as the population grew. Now they are harbingers to the will of the Manastream, granted the special abilities and artes their ancestors once held.

I have awaited the arrival of this child for so many years. I know the path ahead of her and pray for her safety, but I have long since ceased expecting the Gods to reply.

I remain in my chair, daring to contemplate what would become of me if the Gods were no longer, when an alert flashes over my view. A circle lights up in the chair arm and a long cylindrical tube rises from the centre. I bite my tongue, recoiling, and snatch the message from the tube. I stretch it into a silvery piece of paper which twinkles like galaxies and draws my breath as white letters form into words before my eyes.

Oath breaker,

You are called to leave your post and appear before the Guardian Council and stand trial for your infractions.

Failure to do so will be considered an admission of guilt and will result in the termination of you and your planet.

Bile slicks from my throat to my stomachs.

This was it. The notice I have been expecting all these many years.

I close my viewing pane and rise from my chair.

I only hope they will come to see I did it all for my planet. For those under my care.

For Alamantra.

* * *

Acknowledgements

I would like to, as always, start by thanking Craig Hallam for setting me on my creative journey by suggesting I planned a D&D campaign some years back. Through failing miserably to DM, I came to realise I am in fact an author and thus became The Light of Miera. It's also thanks to him I met Amy Wilson, another incredible author, who did an amazing job editing this manuscript.

This book is dedicated to John Jackson, who was a friend to me when I needed one the most. He was fiercely loyal and kind, and so unbelievably talented and creative he managed to rekindle my own passions for art and creativity. I'm sad he never got to see my fully realised series and miss him greatly.

I get to blame Brook Rogers and Geej for this collection, because they encouraged me to go for it when I doubted myself. And for supporting me along this short but intensive project, despite having a million things to deal with in their own lives.

Many thanks as always to my beta readers, Twitch supporters and proof readers who help me improve with every project. Your investment in me and my world is what keeps me motivated and I could not do it without you all.

Finally, to Papa Mash. I know I wasn't the best child growing up and I'm a bit of a disaster adult now, but you love and accept me regardless. Thank you for introducing me to sci-fi and fantasy works and feeding the love of anime and video games which continue to inspire me to this day.

About the Author

Ash Hester started her career in comics and animation, but always had a love for storytelling and fantasy. Contributing to several indie press projects, she later founded Niche: Treat Your Geek to showcase news and reviews featuring the many talented people within her reach. Fuelled by Anime, Television and Video Games, her imagination shows no bounds leading her to begin writing her first epic fantasy novel in 2019. Venturing deeper into the nerd havens of Twitch and Twitter, she found herself welcomed within the D&D and TTRPG community where she featured in several Actual Plays.

If you would like to support her and follow her work, please consider leaving a review of her work on Amazon and Goodreads.

Twitter: www.twitter.com/Author_A_Hester

Website: www.authorahester.uk/

Printed in Great Britain
by Amazon